WILL THE
REAL
ABI
SAUNDERS
PLEASE
STAND UP?

Also by Sara Hantz

IN THE BLOOD

WILL THE REAL ABI SAUNDERS PLEASE STAND UP?

A NOVEL BY

Sara Hantz

Entangled Publishing, LLC
2614 South Timberline Road
Suite 109
Fort Collins, CO 80525
Visit our website at www.entangledpublishing.com.

Edited by Tracy Montoya and Shannon Godwin
Cover design by Kelley York

Print ISBN   978-1-62266-262-3
Ebook ISBN   978-1-62266-263-0

Manufactured in the United States of America

First Edition May 2014

Dedicated to my children, Alicia and Marcus.

Chapter One

"You're kidding, right?" I stare hard at my trainer, Bill, waiting for the usual smirk to appear on his face. I've been kickboxing here at the dojo for eight years, since I was ten, and his practical jokes are legendary. As if he's really fixed it for me to audition as a stunt double for movie star Tilly Watson. As in Tilly Watson. *The Tilly Watson.*

I don't think so.

Although it's not like Bill to call someone to his office just to play a joke, especially during one of the evening classes, since that's when he's so busy. There's always a really good reason if he wants a word in private. And often, the *private* words are the ones you don't want to hear.

I glance around his office at the trophy cabinets bursting with awards for the dojo, going back years. The wall is covered in photos of Bill, when he was younger and had hair, standing with kickboxing champions he'd trained and celebrities who'd come to the gym he used to own in L.A. He's especially proud of his photo with Jackie Chan, from when he consulted on one of Jackie's movies. So, he's got the right connections, that's for sure. But seriously. Me?

"Not kidding this time Abi, I swear." He leans forward in his office chair and makes a little cross over his heart with his forefinger. "My buddy, Danny, is an assistant stunt coordinator, and he told me that Tilly Watson's making an indie movie here in Nebraska, and her regular double has broken her arm. They need to replace her right away. He's trying out some girls for the job, and he asked if I could recommend anyone, since they'd like someone with kickboxing experience. When I told him you took the North American WAKO title at age sixteen, he was hooked." WAKO is the World Association of Kickboxing Organizations. I won the point-fighting women's flyweight youth title in the Pan-America championships last year. "Plus, you'll be perfect. An obvious choice, if you ask me. Identical build and everything."

They must be desperate if they want to audition someone like me. I glance down at the black gym gear I'm wearing, which flattens my chest so much that if you put a bag on my head, you wouldn't know which way I was facing. A far cry from Tilly's enviable size-D cups, which some gossip blogs reported her having surgically enhanced after they saw her coming out of a clinic a few months back.

"S-s-same height, maybe," I argue, my stomach already in knots at the thought of my kickboxing—and my body—being scrutinized by a bunch of Hollywood types. "But that's where the similarity ends. If you haven't noticed, my hair's shoulder-length and blond, and hers is long and dark. Not to mention my nose." My nose has been an issue with me ever since I broke it last year in a bike accident. There's a crooked little bend in it now that mocks me every time I look in the mirror.

"A technicality," Bill says, waving his hand dismissively. "Nothing a wig and make-up can't fix. And, for the record, there's more similarity between you than height. There's shoulder width. The way you stand. After Danny asked me, I watched one of her movies to check her out. There's a definite likeness."

I don't really get what he means, but even if he's right about those things, it doesn't matter, because, more importantly, a wig and make-up can't fix the sheer terror of having to mix with loads of people I've never met before. I might have my stutter mostly under control when I'm with people I know, or when kickboxing, but in a room full of strangers…that's a whole new ball game, even with the breathing techniques that, although haven't cured me, have helped me a lot for so many years. Just the thought of leaving the comfort of the gym for the unknown is making me break out in hives.

Then again, it would mean meeting Tilly. How ridiculous would that be? She was my favorite child movie star when I was growing up. We're almost the same age, though she's a little older, and I used to pretend to be her, when she was Jo in *The Hunter Family*, while playing in my bedroom. Even now, I still love her movies. Especially *It's My Life*, which came out a couple of years ago. She played a girl with a disability. It was based on a true story, and the way she portrayed Dani was so believable, it was like she'd been through something similar in her life. Watching that, I felt a strong connection between us. Felt that she would understand what I had gone through in my struggle to speak like a normal person.

"But why suggest me?" I ask. "Doing stunts involves jumping and swimming and getting blown up and all sorts of other dangerous stuff. They might want someone who can fight, but I'm sure they need more experience than that. Experience that I don't have, being just a kickboxer."

"I wouldn't say *just*. You're the best I've ever trained," Bill says nodding.

My heart skips a beat, and I can feel my cheeks flush. He's never said that before. Coming from him, it's high praise. He's not known for giving compliments.

"Thanks so much," I say.

"Which is why I want you to do this. I think it could give you an insight into a career where you can use your talents. Have you thought about what you want to do once school's out?"

"Not really." I bite on my bottom lip, feeling really lame. There's nothing I'm good at, except kickboxing. I'm not smart, so I didn't even consider applying to a good college. Mom made me apply to the local school, though, to study health science. I'd love to be more like Rupert, my older brother. He always gets top grades. He's a jock, too. But I don't hold that against him. I love him dearly...most of the time. He's just a hard act to follow, especially in the classroom. Lucky for me, he never tried kickboxing. He probably would have been better than me at that, too.

"So what do you have to lose? Go and see Danny. It will do you good to shine somewhere other than on the mat. Danny won't take you on if he doesn't think you can do it. He said it's only for basic stunts and some fight scenes, so I'm sure you'll be fine." He nods his head while running his hand along the silver stubble shadowing his pointed chin. I know his eager expression is supposed to encourage, but all he's doing is scaring the crap out of me.

"I don't know," I say.

"Come on. Give it a shot."

I run my tongue along my bottom lip, while playing

it over in my mind. "Thanks for thinking of me. But…"
I let that "but" trail off. Part of me wants to run in the
opposite direction. But part of me is excited by the
prospect. I guess if it's just kickboxing, I could handle it.
After all, I climbed up to the advanced ranks here at the
dojo pretty quickly.

Except I'd still have to be in a room full of strange
people. And what if they make me actually read lines?

I hold back a shiver.

"Don't say no right away. Give it some thought and
tell me later. If you get the job, Danny will arrange for
someone to train you, and he won't make you do anything that puts you at risk. I promise." Bill gets up from
sitting behind his desk and walks around to where
I'm standing. "And don't worry about your stammer.
You'll be fine. Just remember what you were taught in
the speech program," he says softly. "If you can do this,
you'll be able to do anything. Trust me."

It's easy for him to say; he's not the one who spent
years at school being tormented by the other kids. I
used to dread reading out loud in class so much, I'd be
physically sick on the days my English teacher had us
studying plays.

"I'll think about it," I say, mainly so as not to upset
Bill. He's doing this to help me, I get that.

"Good girl."

I know he means well, and it's not like he doesn't
understand. The reason I came kickboxing here in the

first place was because Mom and I met Bill and his son, who also stutters, at the stutterers' support group we used to go to when I was younger. Bill persuaded Mom that the discipline involved in kickboxing would help in other areas of my life. And he was right. Sort of. At the dojo, everything is cool. Outside? It could be better.

I leave his office and head slowly toward the stairs, my mind a whirr of thoughts. From over the balcony, I notice everyone in my class warming up. The dojo might not be the flashiest building. The furniture is old and has seen better days, same with the carpets. And the paint is peeling in places. But it's clean, the equipment is top of the line, and I love it here. It's where I belong. I quickly scan the room for my best friend Matt. He'll tell me what I should do. Like me, he's a black belt and my go-to for all things kickboxing. What I love about sparring with Matt is that he doesn't think he has to make allowances for me being a girl. Plus, he knows I can whip his ass any time I choose. Even if he does deny it. He's such a typical guy.

Matt's nowhere to be seen, but as I get to the bottom of the stairs, the white entrance door swings open and he comes charging through. He's tall, around six feet, and his lean but muscular frame fills whatever space he's in. He sees me, stops in his tracks, and flashes a wide smile that transforms his dark-and-broody movie star face into something almost boyish.

My heart does a little flip, as usual, when I see him.

He's like Henry Cavill's much better-looking younger brother. But I ignore it. Deep down, I've always had a thing for Matt. He's never felt the same about me, though. Yeah, he flirts, but he does that with everyone. It's part of his DNA, so it doesn't count.

And we're friends. Good friends, and that is what's most important. I've pretty much put my feelings for him in the back of my mind, where they belong. Nothing can happen between us, because it could ruin our friendship. And no way will I ever let that happen.

"Hey, Abi. Not in trouble are you?" He glances up at Bill's office, which is the only room on the second floor. He knows as well as I do that being up there isn't always a good sign.

I move past him and take a place on the mat. "I'll tell you later. Come on, let's warm up before we *do* get in trouble."

"What's with you being so secretive?" he asks as he stretches out his calf muscles.

"I'm not," I say, smirking.

I'm hopeless at keeping anything from him, so I walk away before I break down and tell. Anyway, Bill goes crazy if we stand and chat while we're supposed to be working.

We put on our helmets and face each other. Matt signals for us to start.

As soon as we've finished warming up, I throw the first punch. Matt blocks, kicks back. I block. We fall into the rhythm of the fight. Punch, block, kick. Roundhouse, front kick, block, jab, low kick, hook. And so forth. I throw myself into our sparring, trying not to be distracted by the way his muscles bunch and flex as he does his moves, and almost forget the chance of a lifetime Bill dropped into my lap.

"You're gonna spill, Saunders. And I don't just mean in the ring." Matt grins and winks, his hazel eyes—green mixed with gold—sparkling as he dances back out of my reach.

I snort. As if that's gonna break me.

"So not happening," I yell in his direction. Just in case he thinks he's got a chance.

. . .

"Of course you've got to do it. Why wouldn't you?" Matt asks while we're sitting on the patch of grass outside the dojo. Despite my having toweled off numerous times, sweat is still dripping down my neck and back, staining the neckline of my fitted tank in a very unladylike way. Matt still hasn't cooled down, either, judging by the way his chestnut-brown hair curls damply around his face. We went for each other hard.

"Shut up. You know why not. M-m-m-matt." I exaggerate my stutter to make a point and glare at him, but all he does is pick a blade of grass, put it between his fingers and blow, making a loud squeaky noise.

I roll my eyes toward the sky. He knows how hard things have been for me in the past, so why is he acting like this is an easy decision for me?

"This is Tilly Watson we're talking about." He won't admit it, but from the way he looks when he mentions her name, I figure he's got a crush. "I understand you might be nervous, but this is, like, one chance in a million. You've got to do it." He drops the grass and lifts his head so our eyes meet.

But as for me being her stunt double...

Yes, of course, I'd love to meet Tilly. But I can only imagine what it would be like.

Hi, T-t-t-tilly. N-n-n-n-nice to m-m-meet you.

Yeah, *so* not happening.

"No, Matt. I can't."

"And what does Liv think?"

Liv's my other best friend, and I've known her since grade school. The biggest mistake I ever made was introducing the two of them. They're always ganging up on me, even if it's usually in a nice way.

"She doesn't know."

"If she agrees with me, then you're going to do it. Okay?" He leans across me and picks up the towel, and the sight of his toned six-pack showing underneath the hem of his tight white tee momentarily distracts me. I swear he lets that thing ride up on purpose to see my reaction—or that of any female standing nearby. I shake my head to bring my thoughts back in line.

Well, at least Liv will be on my side. She understands what I went through as a kid. Unlike Matt, I don't have The Abs to mesmerize people with. "Fine. Text her."

He glances up, looking at something over my shoulder. "Already did."

I swing my head around and see Liv's battered green Civic squeal up to the curb. She gets out and slams the door, charging over toward us. *What the…*

"Abi! I can't believe it," she says as she plunks herself and her bag down between Matt and me. "When's the audition?" Her china blue eyes are as wide as her mouth is open.

I can't believe it either. This so isn't what I want to hear. My shoulders sag, and I lean against the big old oak we're sitting under.

"But Liv…" My voice sounds all pathetic and pleading, even to my ears. But it's how I feel.

"Don't even think of telling me you don't want to go," she says sharply.

"You don't understand. This is way too big for me to get my head around." I throw my hands in the air out of sheer exasperation. "I don't know why Bill couldn't have asked someone else."

"Like who?" Matt says. "No one else is remotely at your level. Plus, you're the right age and the right size. An obvious choice, if you ask me."

"What is it with everyone thinking Tilly and I are similar? We're most definitely *not*. And I should know—

I see myself in the mirror every day."

"Look, Abi," Liv says, locking eyes with me. "You've got to put yourself out there. You can't always hide in the shadows. This is your chance to show everyone what you can do." She busts out into a series of stereotypically girly punches to illustrate. I know she means well, but there's a reason field hockey is her thing. "No way are you turning down such an opportunity. Absolutely no way. Is she, Matt?" Liv turns her head in Matt's direction, obviously confident he'll take up where she left off.

It's like she's got a hotline to Bill, practically repeating his every word. If I didn't know better, I'd say that Bill talked to them both before he even approached me to get them on his side. All we'll need now is Mom to get involved, and we'll have triple the fun. I get that they think they're ganging up on me for my own good, but maybe they should leave me alone to make my own decisions. Which I am quite capable of doing. Most of the time.

"A once-in-a-lifetime chance," Matt says. "That's what I've been telling her."

"Exactly," says Liv, folding her arms and subconsciously assuming her I-am-a-wall-and-nothing's-going-to-get-past-me goalie stance.

"Look, if you're so thrilled, then *you* go," I say to Liv. "You'd be much better than me." I conveniently ignore the fact that unless she has a hockey stick in her hand, Liv hits about as effectively as Kermit the Frog. "There's bound to be hundreds of people there. You know what these movie crews are like. Even the assistant to the assistant kitchen hand has an assistant. I'd sooner be fed to sharks than have to face all that."

"That can be arranged," Liv retorts. "Don't underestimate us just because we're in Nebraska." She turns her body toward me and rests her hands on my shoulders. "Look," she continues, her voice slightly more gentle than before. "I'm your best friend, and I know you better than anyone else." She's right about that. I owe her big time. We started school the same day, and I couldn't have coped without her protection from the merciless, teasing bullies. She's been fighting my fights and standing up for me for as long as I can remember. "There's no way it'll be as bad as you imagine. You don't even have to talk to anyone if you don't want to, so don't worry about that. They want you for your kickboxing; just pretend it's one of your matches."

She makes it sound so easy, but then it *would* be for her. She couldn't care less about walking into a room full of strangers and talking to them. I'm feeling beyond sick just thinking about it.

"I suppose that could work." I bite down on the inside of my mouth as I process what she's been saying.

I love Liv to bits, and I know she has my interests at heart, but she'll never know what it's like, however much I try to explain. It's not her fault. You have to experience wanting to say something and not being able to get the words out to know what it feels like.

"Of course it will work," she says. "Just remember, it's only an audition, so it's not like the real thing. You're not going to be faced with all the actors and crew, are you?"

"I guess not." I sigh. Something tells me Liv's already made the decision for me.

"So you'll go?" she asks, her eyes bright with anticipation.

"I'm still not sure," I say.

"Abi, stop it. You can do this. Have some faith in yourself. After all you've been through together, do you really think Bill would ask you if he thought you couldn't?"

"She's right," Matt adds. "If Bill thinks you'll be okay, you will be. Go on. Tell him yes. We'll come with you to the audition if you want."

"Sure," Liv replies, nodding, which causes her dark bangs to fall across her forehead. "It'll be hard having to hang around a movie set with lots of celebs. But I'll be there for you, Abi, because that's the sort of thing best friends do for each other."

She bursts out laughing and Matt follows. I can see I'm fighting a losing battle. I smile at them both—at least I think it's a smile. I'm probably going to regret this, but what the hell.

"Okay. Okay. I'll go." A shiver shoots down my spine, and I'm not sure whether it's from excitement or fear.

Whatever. If this does work out, I can never again complain about my life being boring. Not that I ever do, but just saying.

"Awesome. And just think, when you're famous there'll be a line of guys wanting your number. How cool would that be?" A dreamy expression crosses her face.

Guys all wanting my number, huh? That would be a first. We'd see how many were left standing after I took an hour to recite it to them. I glance across at Matt, to see if the thought of guys wanting to ask me out bothers him at all, but all he's doing is grinning. Probably thinking that I'll be able to introduce him to Tilly. Well, that's definitely not on my agenda.

"I haven't got the job yet," I say. "I've got to audition first. And there's every chance that I'll get there and then make a mad dash away from the place."

"I can assure you, that's not going to happen. I'll be holding your hand every step of the way." She folds her arms tightly across her chest and narrows her eyes, her lips locked together in grim determination. You don't mess with Liv when she's like this. Not if you know what's good for you.

Chapter Two

"Are you sure you don't want me to go with you?" Mom asks as I'm heading out the door to where Matt's waiting to take me to the audition.

We've had this discussion a few times, but I persuaded her that I'll be fine going with Matt. I don't think bringing parents to an audition is a great look for a stunt girl. I'm eighteen, not eight. Liv wanted to come, too, but she had hockey practice.

"I'm sure. I'll call you after."

"Okay. Good luck and break a leg."

I laugh. "Now you've done it. Actors say break a leg instead of good luck, since saying that is *bad* luck."

I'm still smiling to myself as I run down the drive and hop into the car.

Matt starts the engine, and we take off down the road with a squeal of tires. Matt owns an old BMW, and he likes to push it to its limits.

"How do you feel?" he asks, fast approaching a Honda Civic that seems to be creeping along at just under the speed limit.

"I've had better days," I say. "And Matt, slow down! Unless you want to kill me before my audition and put me out of my misery."

He hits the brakes, and a gap forms between us and the car ahead. I check the side mirror and relax my tense muscles. Thank goodness there's no one close behind, or we'd have been in trouble.

"Sorry," he says.

"Well, keep your eyes on the road and not on the girl in the car next to us," I say shaking my head.

"What girl?" We come to a stop next to a small blue hatchback, but the blond ponytail I'd glimpsed on the driver turns out to belong to a woman who has to be at least in her forties. Oops. "I wasn't looking at a girl," Matt continues. "I just don't want you to be late. It makes you tense."

Okay, so maybe I misjudged him. This time. He knows that there's an anal time-keeping gene in my family, which I inherited, and we are never late for anything. As in *never*. It drives Matt and Liv crazy at times, since they're much more relaxed about time than me.

I glance down at my waterproof Armitron watch—

one I can sweat all over at the gym without busting it—which isn't exactly at the height of fashion. "The audition isn't for another thirty minutes." And the studio, where I'm meeting this Danny character, is only about ten minutes away.

"In my world, you have plenty of time. In Abi world, we're almost late," says Matt. "And, knowing you, you'll need the bathroom to freshen up."

"Throw up, more like," I mutter. For the last two days, I've eaten virtually nothing and spent the time in a permanent state of panic. My concentration's been totally shot, even at the dojo. I've played over and over in my mind how I think it's going to go and am convinced that I'm going to be a total screw up. Doing choreographed fight scenes for a movie isn't kickboxing. It's never gonna be kickboxing. So what the hell was I on when I agreed to try it? How many more times in my life do I have to look like a fool? Bile rises in my throat. I've made a big mistake.

"I can't do it, Matt. I'm sorry. Turn the car around."

Matt pulls over to the curb and turns to face me. He takes my hand in his and gives it a squeeze, causing my stomach to knot. I remind myself it's only done in friendship, nothing else. "Don't back out now. It's just nerves, and they'll go once it starts. Let's sit here for a few minutes and talk about something totally unrelated to the audition."

Just looking at the concerned expression on his face

soothes my nerves a little. He has this way of grounding me.

"Okay," I say, glancing down at our still-joined hands and then back up at him. "How's Selina?"

Selina is his latest girlfriend. Not that he sees her often, since he spends so much time at the dojo and with Liv and me.

"We're not together any more. She wanted me to meet her parents. And you know I don't do that."

I certainly do. As far as he's concerned, meeting the parents means the relationship is serious. And the one thing he doesn't want is a serious relationship. This is why he can never know how I feel about him. Girlfriends come and go for Matt. And he flirts like there's no tomorrow. With friends he's different. As a friend, there's no one more reliable or true than Matt. He's always got your back. No way am I going to risk that.

"Another one bites the dust," I say arching an eyebrow.

"Yep." He looks at his own sports watch, the guy's version of mine. "So are you going to go to the audition, or…?"

I tell myself to stop being stupid and to suck it up. Because if I don't do this, then the next time something comes along I might not do that either. I don't mean another movie audition, because that's hardly likely, but anything else.

"Okay, I'll go. Because when they turn me down, which they will, no one, a.k.a. you and Liv, will be able to moan at me for not giving it my best shot."

I sit up straight in the seat and draw in what an old speech therapist once called "a positive breath." I can do this. I can.

"Good. Because you're gonna kill it." Matt turns on the engine and pulls out into the road.

We drive for another few minutes then he turns into the studio parking lot. He parks and practically leaps out of the car while I take my time. Zodiac Studios, where they're holding the audition, is a small office-type building that looks about ready to be demolished. It's gray brick, and I count five floors. Fire escape stairs snake down the east wall of the building, facing us. It seems pretty deserted. There are only two other cars parked there. We head toward the main entrance.

Before I can change my mind and decide to remain in the car indefinitely, the passenger-side door swings open, and Matt tugs me out. He then propels me to the studio's front entrance. *Can't be any harder than a tournament match, right?*

"I'll go the rest of the way on my own," I announce, shaking him off before he can reach for the door handle.

"Why don't I go in with you?" he asks, biting his full lower lip with concern.

"Thanks, but I don't know if it's allowed."

His green-and-gold eyes fix on mine, and he starts

running his palms up and down my shoulders, looking as if he wants to say something. But he doesn't. He breaks contact and shrugs. "Okay. I'll see you back at the car."

After watching Matt stroll across the parking lot, I push open the door and follow the red arrows on the sign saying reception.

The reception area turns out to be just a small room with a glass window that has a space underneath to talk through. An old woman is sitting at a desk behind the window speaking on the phone. She mouths "one minute," and I take a step away so she doesn't think I'm trying to listen. Though it's hard not to hear everything she says since her voice is really loud. My ears prick up when she mentions Danny's name and tells the caller he has an appointment this afternoon but should be free in about an hour, maybe less.

That's strange. How many people is he going to be able to see in an hour? Not many. Unless we're auditioning as a group. I hope so. A group audition, with any luck, won't require me to speak as much.

"Abi Saunders?" The sound of the woman's voice cuts across my thoughts.

"Um, yes." I frown. How does she know my name before I've even spoken?

"You're a little early." Tell me something I don't know. It's the story of my life. "So, if you take a seat over there." She points to a threadbare red-striped sofa crammed against the opposite wall. "Danny will be with you as soon as he can."

"Thanks."

"The bathroom is through the double doors, first door on the right," she adds as I walk away.

The bathroom is in the same state of disrepair as the rest of the place. There's an old white sink with green stains down the back from where water has dripped, and the taps look so rusty, it wouldn't surprise me if they didn't turn at all. The room isn't dirty. Just old. I don't know what I expected for a film studio but not something like this. Then again, Bill did say Zodiac is an indie studio—which it would have to be, being located in Nebraska of all places—so they won't have the money they do for the big blockbuster Hollywood movies.

I glance at my reflection in the cracked mirror. Big mistake. My skin's devoid of any color. I pinch my cheeks a few times, and they become pinker. If only I could fix my pounding heart so easily. Some more deep breathing may do the trick. I often do deep breathing before matches, to get myself in the zone.

After a few more minutes, and feeling calmer than before, I go back to the reception. Just in time, because as soon as I push open the door, the old woman speaks.

"Here she is. Abi, this is Danny."

Danny's so tall I have to strain my neck to look up at him. He must be close to seven feet. The opposite of Bill, who I can look square in the eye since he's only about five feet six. Danny's six-pack shows through his dark red tee. He must work out for hours every day. He's not even that young. Looks about the same age as Dad, and he's forty-five.

He strides over to meet me.

"Hello, Abi. Good to meet you." He smiles, and it doesn't come off as cheesy and fake like a stereotypical Hollywood producer—it lights up his whole face. He holds out his hand for me to shake, leaning down slightly in the process.

"H-h-hi." I shake his hand and curse inside my head for not even managing to get one word out without stuttering. I draw in some deep breaths without being too obvious to try and calm myself down.

"I don't know what Bill told you, but we need a stunt double for Tilly to start 'yesterday,' since our original girl injured herself. She's done a lot of the more difficult stunts, but we still have quite a few choreographed fight scenes left. Bill has told me great things about you. His star student." He grins. I smile back weakly. "Right. Let's get started." He rubs his hands together. "Is Studio One okay, Jean?" Danny calls over to the old woman, or Jean, as I now know her. She glances down.

"For the next forty-five minutes, then Dave wants it."

"Thanks, we should be out by then. C'mon Abi."

I follow Danny through the double doors and down a long corridor. Eventually, we get to Studio One. It's smaller than I'd imagined and is bare except for five cameras surrounding the big wooden floor. There's a guy standing beside one of the cameras.

"Make yourself at home," Danny says after introducing me to the camera guy. "Take five minutes to warm up."

"O-o-okay."

I go to the back of the studio floor and take off my shoes and jeans. Underneath, I wore my black leggings, as roundhouse and axe kicks are too hard to do in jeans. Not that I know whether he wants me to do any. I just wanted to be prepared.

I begin to relax while I'm doing my warm-up stretching exercises. It's just like being in class. I can do this.

I glance up and see Danny talking to the camera guy, who then wheels the camera to about three feet away from me.

"Ignore us," Danny says. "We're just setting up. Tell us once you've finished, and we'll start recording."

That's easier said than done. How am I expected to ignore them when they're so close. As in, *in my bubble* close?

I pull my right arm across my chest, stretching my triceps and shoulder muscles. I take my time warming up, and not just because I'm procrastinating—the last thing I want is an injury. There's a match in a few weeks that I need to be one-hundred percent fit for if I'm going to take the trophy. Because I sure as heck don't think I'll be cast in Tilly's movie.

"I-I-I'm r-r-r-ready," I say after a few minutes.

"Are you okay?" He frowns and looks in my direction.

Oh, God, didn't Bill tell him?

The mixture of concern and puzzlement in Danny's eyes is far from reassuring, because it takes me back to how the teachers used to be at school, when my stammer was bad. They tried to hide it, but I could see their impatience at having to wait for me to say the words. It was mortifying.

"U-u-u-um, y-y-yes. I th-th—." I want to curl up behind one of the cameras and die. Why did I let Liv and Matt talk me into doing this? I should have gone with my gut and said no. I know my limits. "I th-th-think s-s-s—"

With a glance at the cameraman, who is making a big show of adjusting his equipment, Danny walks over to me and sits down on the floor, patting the space in front of him. I gladly give up on finishing my sentence and join him. "I'm sorry," he says quietly, obviously trying not to embarrass me in front of the camera guy. "But maybe you're not right for this. Bill said you have the technical skills, but there's a certain"—he waves his hand in the air, trying to conjure the right word—"*confidence* that Tilly has, that her stunt double also needs in order to pull it off. I don't think it's going to work, Abi."

My jaw drops. He's handing me the chance to back

out. Well, not the chance, he's actually made the decision for me. Except I'm not sure it's what I want. I've spent years trying to control my stammer and not let it control my life, and here's one situation out of the ordinary, and I lose it. I'm suddenly possessed by the feeling that I can't let this happen.

"L-let me try. Please," I say, relieved that most of the words came out on the first attempt.

"Well—"

I push myself to my feet, putting my weight in my toes, my hands curved into loose fists. "I won the region-al kickboxing championship after my first two years at the dojo, and Bill's already told you about me winning the WAKO Pan America youth title in my weight class. I'm here because I can fight." Wow, I have no idea where that came from. "You did need someone 'yesterday,' r-r-right?"

He stares at me for what seems like forever, then jumps up. "Okay, as long as you're here. What's the harm?"

He seems like a nice guy, just doing his job, I guess. Well, I'm gonna show him what I can do. If he doesn't want me after that, then I know it's for the right reasons and not because I can't talk.

"Thanks." The word comes out fine, and I feel my confidence return.

"First of all, I need to see if you could pass for Tilly on screen from the different angles we'll be shooting. Ignore the camera. I don't have a set routine for you,

I'm more concerned with how you look. So just show us some of your kickboxing moves. Include some jumps, and use as much of the floor space as possible."

But we don't do jumps, apart from jumping jacks during the warm up. I bite on my bottom lip and think. My mind's a total blank until, suddenly, I remember the sparring exhibition we did a couple months ago at the Woodrow Center. Matt and I were partners, but I could do my side of things, which involves lots of punching, kicking, and blocking.

Yes! That should be perfect.

I force all thoughts of Danny and the camera out of my mind and launch into the exhibition routine, and luckily it comes back to me almost instinctively as I go. Hardly surprising as we practiced it so often I could do it in my sleep. I make a couple of tiny mistakes, but hopefully it doesn't matter. It's not like I'm scoring points here. It's hard not to notice the camera, though. It feels like I'm being stalked by a Dalek from *Doctor Who*.

At the end of the routine, Danny and the camera guy applaud. Does he mean it, or is he feeling guilty for what he said earlier, and he just wants me to feel good?

"Was that okay?" I ask, scanning Danny's face.

"More than okay. You're a natural. Like two different people on and off screen. You know, the camera loves you—come and look." A tingling feeling washes over me. He can't be serious. Me, a natural?

I run over to where he's standing behind the camera looking at a small screen, and he replays my screen test.

If you don't count my face, which by the end of it is all red and sweaty, the actual routine looks great. I'm not sure I'd say I'm a natural, though. Not that I know what counts as one. Even so, I'd love to have a copy of it to take home and show everyone, not that I have the nerve to ask.

"Thanks. And thank you for seeing me."

Danny starts to roll the camera away toward the side of the studio, and I pull on my jeans and shoes. Once I'm back in my street clothes, I head for the door.

"Hey, where are you going?" Danny calls.

I turn and walk back toward him, chewing on my bottom lip. I hope he doesn't think I'm rude. "S-sorry, I thought we'd finished."

"I want to explain the process. I've already seen a couple of other girls earlier and now I have to talk to the casting director, and we'll make a decision and let you know later."

"Okay. Thanks."

For some reason, I feel a bit deflated. But the main thing is that I did it and that my nerves didn't get the better of me. It's not like I expected to be offered the job on the spot. That only happens in the movies. But now that I'm here, and the audition is over, my dread is that I'll go home and receive the *thanks but no thanks* call because they've decided on someone more suitable. Which is one-hundred percent going to happen, no matter how much I want the job now. I have no experience, and that's the beginning and end of it, even if Bill did persuade him to test me. So I should stop daydreaming about how exciting working on a movie would be and just accept that my chances are slim, if that.

"You haven't asked me anything about the job. Don't you have any questions?" Danny asks.

"Sorry." *Question. Think of a question.* "Um. Can you tell me more about the movie?"

"Sure. What do you know about New Zealand?"

Help. I've never been good at geography. Hope it's not going to affect my chances if I tell him I haven't a clue. Then again, it's not like it will determine how well I do the stunts, if they want me.

"Not much. Sorry." In other words, nothing apart from the fact that it's where they shot the *Lord of the Rings,* and it's a long way from here.

"No matter." He leans back in his chair. "Most people think of Nebraska as flat, but in fact parts of Omaha, especially the Loess Hills, are similar to New Zealand's hills, which is why we chose to shoot there. The movie's loosely based on the ancient Maori legend of Mataaho, but with a more contemporary feel."

Contemporary feel? How do you make legends contemporary?

I look down at my lap and notice I'm flicking the

nail of my middle finger with my thumb. I quickly stop. Mom gets mad at me when I do it. She says the clicking noise is really annoying.

"Cool." What else can I say? "And what part does Tilly play?"

"Princess Waiere. Hunua's daughter. She falls in love with Hui and runs away with him to his tribe. According to the legend, the God of Secrets and his brother got really angry with a high priest of the tribe the princess came from for stealing magic and using it to fight Hui's tribe. The Gods killed the high priest and turned the ground into volcanoes."

"When you say it's going to be contemporary, do you mean it's not set in fairyland?"

"Not as such. It's still going to be a fantasy, but it's a twenty-first-century fairyland."

"What?" I clamp my hand across my mouth. I didn't mean for that to come out.

Danny frowns. "It may sound strange, but it's a good script. And story. You've got to remember we're appealing to a world-wide audience, and most of them won't know anything about Maori culture."

Like me, he means.

"I suppose," I say, slowly shaking my head. "And what sort of stunts will I be doing? I-I-I mean will the stunt person be doing?"

"Oh, the usual. Fighting mostly, which is where being able to kickbox comes into play and why we need someone with your talent. There will also be some wirework. And motorcycle scenes."

He talks for five more minutes and then walks me to the door. My head's spinning with it all as I make my way over to the car where Matt is waiting.

I actually survived the audition and didn't make a total ass of myself. Who knew?

CHAPTER THREE

Matt parks outside the entrance of Chelsea's, our favorite café, where we've arranged to meet Liv. While he goes to the counter, I find us a table by the window and stare out of it, looking but not really seeing as I think about the audition and how I persuaded Danny to let me try out. If I do get the job, then it's not going to be easy. Not the kickboxing side of things. That I'm comfortable with. But the rest. That will be tough. The constant pressure to monitor myself and my breathing before speaking can be really draining.

I glance across at Matt waiting in line. He's wearing my favorite blue tee, which sets off his eyes. He looks so good in that color. His chestnut-brown hair is all tousled, like someone just ran her fingers through it. He flashes a smile to the girl behind the counter, and she blushes and smiles back at him. Whatever.

"Here you are," Matt says as he walks over to me.

He places the tray on the table. There are coffees and muffins for the three of us, and a panini.

"I take it the panini is for you?" I ask.

With Matt, his stomach is always first. I've never known anyone who eats as much as he does. And he always finishes anything Liv and I can't. It has to be seen to be believed.

He laughs, then pulls his hoodie over his head and hangs it over the back of his chair. He drags his hand through his hair, attempting to flatten it, but it still sticks out in all directions. He hates it. I think it's cute. But, of course, he doesn't know that. No one does.

We wait another fifteen minutes for Liv. She sees us and waves, absentmindedly swinging a sheet of long, dark hair away from her eyes. She treats us to a wide smile that belongs in a teeth-whitening commercial. Despite the fact that she probably just got out of field hockey practice, she looks perfect.

"Hey," she says when she reaches the table. "Sorry, I'm late." She pulls out the chair opposite me and sits down. "Hockey practice went on and on. For some reason, coach decided we're all unfit and got us doing speed drills until we collapsed. What a nightmare, especially since all I wanted to do was find out how it went today." She fans herself with her hand.

"No problem," I say, laughing at her.

"So, tell me everything," Liv says excitedly. "What was the audition like? How many other girls were there? Did you see Tilly? Was Danny hot? What was the studio like? How did you…?"

"Stop." I cut her off and hold up my hand. "One question at a time, please." There's no stopping her when she gets on a roll. She gets so involved, it's like it's happening to her.

"Sorry." She giggles.

"First, no Tilly wasn't there, thank goodness, or I'd have freaked, big time. And second, Danny was nice for an older guy. And third…"

"And third, she killed it," Matt says, nudging me with his elbow.

"I nailed the routine, if that's what you mean." I nudge him back, smiling up at him.

"As if you wouldn't." He wraps his arm around my shoulder and gives it a squeeze. His fingers idly stroke my neck.

My stomach does a little flip. Do friends do that sort of thing to each other? Of course they do, if they're Matt. Stupid, over-friendly, touchy-feely Matt. There's nothing in it. I'm just allowing my imagination to get the better of me, again. But, whatever. It feels nice.

"Did you have any problems with…you know…?" Liv asks.

The stuttering elephant, she means, that's always in

the room.

"At first. I nearly blew it before the audition even started. But I guess it could've been much worse. I could've totally screwed up the routine, too."

"So overall, everything was fine," Liv says. "See, I told you it would be." She does a little dance in her seat.

Warmth radiates through me. After all the stress of today, it's just nice to be alone with Liv and Matt. I don't have to worry about speaking and not getting the words out. I don't have to worry about anything. I can just be myself.

"I guess," I reply.

"When do you hear back?" Liv asks.

"I don't know. Danny said he'd call when they've made a decision. But, to be honest, I don't care what happens. I got through the audition, which is more than I thought would happen yesterday. Not to mention, can you really imagine me working on a movie? It's what dreams are made of, and we all know dreams are dreams and reality is reality."

"Stop the crazy talk," Liv says. "You have just as much right to your dreams coming true as the rest of us."

She's right, except working in the movies has never been my dream. I don't really have real dreams, apart from the obvious—to never stutter again. Oh…and to win the world championship next year. Okay, so I do have dreams.

"I hear you," I say. "Anyway, no more talk about the

audition, because whatever we say won't affect the out-come."

"Ah, that's where you're wrong," Liv says. "You have to tell the universe that you want the job. Then it will happen. So we all have to put out positive vibes. That means you too, Matt."

Matt rolls his eyes toward the ceiling. He has no time for Liv's "hippy-dippy stuff," as he calls it.

"Ridiculous," he says, leaning back in his chair and folding his arms tightly across his chest.

Liv reaches across and smacks him on the head—lightly, but enough for him to know she means business. She sits back and focuses her determined gaze on me. Uh-oh.

"I, Abi Saunders," she says, palms in the air like she's meditating, "want to be a stunt double in this movie with Tilly Watson. I want this job, therefore I will have this job. Repeat."

"Really, Liv?" I say.

My cell, vibrating on the table, suddenly captures my attention. I go to pick it up when it stops. I'd put it on silent for the audition and forgotten to turn the ringer back on. Who would be calling me? It can't be Mom, because I already called her. And the only other people who call me are sitting right here. Except—

After a few seconds a message comes in.

"It's Danny," I say after listening to it. I wasn't ex-pecting to hear from him so soon. "He wants me to call."

Beads of sweat form on my forehead and a mass of thoughts swirl around my head. Is it yes? Is it no? Why couldn't he just tell me in the message? Does he want to see me again? Is he just contacting me because he's friends with Bill and wants to let me down gently?

"To offer you the job," Liv exclaims. "I knew it. The universe is listening, as it always does."

Matt makes sounds that resemble a cat in distress to express his feelings about Liv's comment.

"We don't know that. He's Bill's friend, and a nice guy, so maybe he wants to tell me in person that I didn't get it."

"Call him now," Liv demands. "The not knowing is driving me crazy."

"Not here," I say. It seems stupid, but what if I start to cry when he tells me no? Which, first of all, is hardly what you'd expect of someone my age and, second of all, is just plain embarrassing. "I think I'll go outside and do it."

"I'm coming with," Liv says, jumping up and following me, not giving me a chance to object.

I glance back at Matt who is watching us leave. I hope he doesn't mind being left there on his own. Actually, why would he? He's a guy.

Once we're outside, I swallow hard and then call Danny. He answers after the first ring.

"Abi. Thanks for getting back to me. I wanted to let you know we've looked at all the screen tests, and we'd like to offer you the role of stunt double for Tilly."

My jaw drops. "I-I-I've got the j-job?" My voice is barely above a whisper as the enormity of Danny's words hit me. "E-e-even though I've n-n-never done stunt work before?"

Pinch me someone now. This just isn't happening to me.

"Even though," he says gently. "Because it didn't stop you outclassing the professionals we auditioned, plus your likeness on screen to Tilly is uncanny."

Is he serious? I beat out the professionals. How the heck did I do that?

"You do want the job, I take it?" Danny's voice breaks my train of thought.

Good question. Unfortunately, the answer eludes me at this precise moment. I thought I did, but that was before. Now my mind's pure mush. "Um, well…"

My heartbeat quickens. What if I say *yes*? Deep down it's what I want. And what's the worst that can happen?

Worst case scenario: I screw up, Bill—someone I've admired for years—thinks I'm the biggest loser to ever walk the planet, I ruin the reputation of the dojo, and Danny will never listen to Bill again.

Crap.

Make that triple crap.

I've always hated making decisions. Hardly surprising when considering my star sign is Libra, and anyone who knows anything about astrology will know what I mean. There's a very good reason why Libra is represented by scales. We're too busy weighing things to decide. Crap, crap, crap, crap, crap…

On the other hand, as Mom would say, the world won't come to an end if I give it a shot and it doesn't work out.

"Yes, please," I finally say to Danny.

A rush of adrenaline shoots through me. I've just said yes. I must be crazy.

"Cool," he replies.

He spends the next few minutes going over the main things in my contract and says he'll email it to me so I can sign it.

"Thanks," I say when he finishes.

We say goodbye, and I glance at Liv who's double punching the air.

"Yes!" she shouts, flinging her arms around me, giving me the hugest of hugs.

"Okay," I say, gasping for air. "If you squeeze me any tighter, the only thing I'll be fit for is corpse-double." Liv quickly releases me and lets her arms drop to her side. But she can't stand still; she's jumping all over the place. I'd love to be able to match her excitement, but instead it's fear that's coursing through my veins.

"This is going to be the most insane summer ever. Did he say anything about getting your SAG card? Because that would be so cool."

"Yeah. I have to apply for one after I've been working for thirty days." I shrug, not sure why she thinks a Screen Actors Guild card is such a big deal.

"You do know what that means?"

"What?"

"It's your passport to working on other movies. This is so wasted on you. Why, oh why did I not beg to take kickboxing classes when I was younger?" She folds her arms across her chest and shakes her head, her eyes twinkling.

I burst out laughing. "Lucky for me you didn't."

"Well, I'm going to enjoy movie life through you, instead. Please say I can come to the set sometimes. I'll keep out the way. You won't even know I'm there."

"Ha! Yeah, right." Liv is far from subtle. "If there's any way I can get you on set I will, but I can't promise anything. Not until I know how this whole movie thing works."

"I know that." She gives me her "serious" look. "How much are they paying you?"

"I don't know. Megabucks, I hope." I hadn't even thought about the money until now. Now that I am, how awesome would it be to have a stash of cash?

"You could use the money for our vacation."

We've always dreamed of going overseas, ever since Liv's older sister worked her way across Europe—at one point, she even sheared sheep to make some money. Can't say I want to get up close and personal with livestock, but there's bound to be something for us to do. Liv wants to work behind a bar, but I don't, unless she serves the drinks and I wash up. That would work.

"Yes, that's one option. Or I could buy a car. That would save me relying on Mom for rides, which is definitely something worth considering."

"Good idea. Your mom is the worst driver on the planet. No offense," Liv adds.

"None taken." What Liv says is true. Not that Mom realizes, of course, but I swear last week she almost took out three crossing guards in under five minutes.

I turn to head back into the café.

"I can't wait to tell everyone about the movie. They'll be so freaked," Liv says as she opens the door and we walk back inside.

"NO!" I shout it too loudly, and some girls standing in line stop talking and turn their heads in our direction. "No," I repeat, more quietly. "I don't want anyone else to know."

"Why? This could be our passport into the in-crowd and beyond."

"And we want to be in the in-crowd because?" My lips twitch as I try to maintain a serious face. I know exactly why she wants a higher profile.

"You mean apart from being noticed by Austin?" Liv replies.

Austin is this guy from a local school that Liv thinks is really hot. Trouble is, he doesn't seem to know she exists. If we ever see him at parties, he's surrounded by cheerleading girls. Matt knows him because they're at the same school—he doesn't like him much. He figures Austin thinks he's God's gift to girls. Austin should be so lucky.

"Look, I haven't signed my contract yet. And if I screw this up and they let me go, I'm gonna look like an idiot, so the fewer people who know the better." I keep walking toward our table, with Liv close behind.

"Abi, will you stop it?" Liv demands as we reach Matt. "They wouldn't have offered you the job if they didn't think you could do it."

"You got the job." Matt leaps to his feet and throws his arms around me. "Awesome. Let's celebrate. Cake anyone?"

Everything goes to back to food with Matt. I relax into his hold until suddenly remembering something that Danny told me. Crap. I hope Matt doesn't mind too much. I pull away from him and focus on the floor.

"Yeah, well, before we do, you might want to know that from now on, I'm not allowed to attend class. I can go to the dojo, but I can't do any kickboxing, in case I injure myself. I'm really sorry, but I can't compete with you in the Worthington Trophy again this year." My shoulders sag, at the sadness I feel about having to miss all the extra time we spend together when we're training for something special.

"That's cool," Matt says without missing a beat, but

there's a strange expression on his face that makes me pause. However, the look's gone in an instant, and I wonder if it was all in my imagination.

Chapter Four

"Abi, for God's sake, concentrate," Zac, the director, shouts. "Fairies don't look like elephants when they fly. Legs together, arms graceful, and glide. *Please*."

My cheeks are crimson, and I want to die. We must have gone over this move fifty times already, and I still can't get it. I know, without even looking, that the other guys have lost it with me. It's easy for them, but I'm a kickboxer, not a freakin' acrobat. It's not like I'm not trying my hardest. But the more Zac shouts at me, the harder it is for me to do what he asks. Surely he must realize that.

Now he's saying something to Danny. Let's all guess what it is: *Get rid of the silly girl. We couldn't get anyone more incompetent if we tried. In fact, a monkey could do better.*

Well, a monkey *could* do better. Then again, a monkey wouldn't need to fly across the room wearing a harness that cuts badly into its thighs. We're doing wirework, the one thing I couldn't wait to do. Ha. Well, it looks like the joke's on me.

At least we're not filming yet. This is just the rehearsal or, as they say, "prepping." We're in one of the studios that's full of equipment with pulleys and wires. I have no idea how it all works, except that it keeps me up in the air. They film wirework indoors against a blue screen, and then edit to make it look like it's outside by dropping in a background.

According to Vince, Hui's stunt double, what I'm doing is really basic stuff, nothing like the things they did on *The Avengers*. Which it wouldn't be, obviously, or they'd have employed a real stunt person and not me. I remember reading that the actors had months of training even though many of the stunts were done by stunt doubles. It might be basic for someone who's experienced, like Vince, but it's not for me.

Right. This is it. I'm going to really concentrate. I will not be beaten. I can do this. It's not hard.

I'm a graceful fairy,

I'm a graceful fairy,

I'm a graceful fairy.

"Ready," I call, for the first time feeling confident of success. I'm focused. My body is in the right position, and my head is in the right space.

The technician holds up his thumb so I know we're about to go. I try to relax my mind, then point my toes, bring my legs together, and hold out my arms at forty-five degree angles. So far, so good. I swallow hard as I begin to move exactly as I've been instructed to.

I'm doing it. I'm actually doing it. *Please let Zac say it's okay.*

"Hoo-flipping-ray," booms Zac's voice. "At last, she's got it."

I've done it. I've actually done it. I can now do wirework. And even Zac's sarcastic tone can't spoil it. Matt will be so jealous. Well, not as jealous as when I first told him about the motorcycles I'll be riding, but this will come in a close second. I'll be able to tell him later, because he's been waiting for me at the studio nearly every afternoon this week to see how my day has been and to give me a ride home. I love that he's doing that. Even if it is because he's my friend, and not because he has feelings for me like I have for him…

Put them away, I remind myself. Matt runs in the opposite direction when girls get too serious. The last thing I want him to do is run from our friendship, so I lose him forever.

A loud crash, sounding like someone slamming the door, gives me a start, and I jerk backwards. My legs splay, and I lose all control of my body, until suddenly I'm hanging upside down.

This so isn't happening to me. My hair flops in front of my eyes, and my arms dangle in mid-air. Let's not even think about how shallow my breathing is.

Crap.

After what seems like an eternity (which is probably only a few seconds), someone starts a slow handclap. And here's me thinking it couldn't get any worse.

I figure it's Zac and wait for everyone to join in. Except they don't.

The silence is deafening. Until…

"Look at that stupid girl. What is she doing?"

Oh, no. That voice is a dead ringer for Tilly's. But it can't be. I know this is her first day back on set since I've started, but Vince said earlier that she's filming in the hills today, a good hour's drive from here. More to the point, I'm in no rush to meet her just yet. I don't want to do that until I've at least come to grips with some of this stuff, or she'll think I'm a total idiot. That so can't happen.

I crane my neck in an attempt to get a better view but still can't see anything other than the wall, and it feels like my neck is going to part ways with the rest of my body.

Don't be her. Don't be her.

Desperate for a better look, I twist my body slightly and swing my arms back and forth, until I start to move. Once I can touch the wall, I give a hard push. Except I'm stronger than I think, and I begin to swing from side to side so fast it makes me feel really sick.

There's no way I can allow myself to throw up on the people below, so I clamp my hand over my mouth. I can't think about that now.

As I continue swinging, I keep getting fleeting glimpses of very dark hair and a pink top that definitely weren't there before.

My mantra of *don't be her* plays on repeat in my head.

After what feels like forever, they pull me to the side where I grab hold of the scaffolding with both hands and pull my legs around so I'm in a standing position.

One of the tech guys reaches over from the platform and unclips me. I just about manage a nod of thanks before he turns around and climbs back down. Other than that I remain motionless. My legs feel like jelly, and I don't dare move in case they give way.

"Okay, everyone," Zac says. "Let's break for lunch. Meet back here in half an hour for a final run through."

Not again, surely. Why? I did it right, didn't I? Zac said so just before the spinning incident.

"You coming, Abi?" Vince calls.

Vince is so nice. Especially to me, right from the first day of rehearsal. And he doesn't make me feel like an idiot for stuttering. In fact, I hardly stutter around him now.

"Sure, I'm on my way." I turn around, take hold of

the sides of the ladder, and climb down. When I get to the bottom and both my feet are safely on the ground, I turn to face them. "Okay, let's…"

My jaw drops to the floor, and my eyes are riveted on HER. As in Tilly Watson. Who is standing next to Zac.

Which means I'm who she was talking about.

Actually, let me rephrase that. I'm the *stupid girl* she referred to.

She won't want me to be her double, now. And after seeing me dangling upside down like I don't know how to fly, I can hardly blame her for having zero faith in me. I so wanted to make a good impression. Even imagined we could be friends. Not right away, but once she got to know me. What are the odds now, though?

Before I can even attempt to drag my eyes off her, Zac looks across and sees me staring. Blood rushes up my face until it's burning hot and, I'm guessing, crimson.

"Abi. Over here." Zac beckons with his hand, then turns his attention back to Tilly, who doesn't even look in my direction.

Crap, crap, crap, crap.

"I'll catch up," I say to Vince. "Will you get me a sandwich and Diet Coke, please?"

How can I think of food at a moment like this? Tilly Watson, movie star, basically announced to everyone that she didn't want me in this movie.

I hitch in a breath, the rush of air hitting the pit of

my stomach and making me shiver. I smooth down my top, which is all twisted from the wirework, and take a purposeful step in the direction of Zac and Tilly. In my head, I try to convince myself everything will be okay, however much my heart is pounding violently against my ribcage.

"Abi." Zac's impatient voice makes me jump. "Hurry up."

"Sorry." I take another step toward him and trip over nothing. Luckily, I manage to right myself before landing splat in front of them both. I take a couple more steps and stand next to Zac.

My eyes are drawn like magnets to Tilly. Not a pimple on her skin, and her hair is sleek and shiny. How does she do it? It's insane that she looks exactly the same in person as she does on screen.

No airbrushing needed with her.

"Tilly, meet Abi your stunt double. Abi, meet Tilly," Zac says.

"H-h-h-hi T-T-Tilly." Help! This isn't happening to me. How hard is it to say hi to someone? But of course I know the answer to that one. Still, maybe she didn't notice. Or will just think that I'm still suffering from being on the wire.

Tilly stares at me, an incredulous expression on her face. "H-h-h-h-h-hiii." She smirks.

I go cold. It's like stepping back in time to elementary school. Being older doesn't make the teasing any easier to deal with, especially since Liv isn't here to stand up for me.

"Tilly, behave," Zac warns narrowing his eyes.

Except it's all for show since he then winks at her. Just because I stutter doesn't make me stupid. I know what they're thinking.

"Whatever," Tilly says rolling her eyes toward the ceiling. "Remember, you're here to make me look good," she adds.

"I-I-I do. I mean I-I-I know. I will. S-s-sorry."

If the earth would open up and swallow me whole right now, it wouldn't be a moment too soon.

"I want you to spend some time with Tilly this afternoon," Zac says.

"W-w-what about the run through?" I ask, remembering he wants us back in half an hour.

"We'll manage without you. For now, stick with Tilly. Watch how she moves, how she stands. Anything you think might help."

Tilly directs a carefully blank look in my direction. Somehow, that's even worse than the irritation she showed before. "You need to get it right. You're supposed to be a *professional*." She turns and walks away.

Well, I could have told them that offering me this job was the craziest thing ever. But I'd hoped the fact they actually wanted *me* meant I had something to offer. That maybe, just maybe, I was special.

Ha! Right now I feel like a hopeless, *unprofessional*

failure.

I clench my teeth to try and stop the tears that are so close to falling. Then give myself a mental slap. I can't give up at the first hurdle. Yes, Tilly was being insensitive. But I've had worse throughout my life. I'm going to ignore what she said and prove to her that I can do a good job.

...

"Tilly, are you in here?" I call, opening the bathroom door.

I've been searching everywhere, but it seems that she's nowhere to be found. I'd give up except for Zac's instructions. I don't want to get on his bad side. Vince figures Tilly's giving me the run around on purpose. I don't know why, not if she wants me to make her look good.

"Can't a girl pee in peace?" Tilly snaps, her voice coming from one of the cubicles on the left.

Ah ha. I've found her.

"S-s-sorry. I'll wait outside for you."

Tilly mutters something that I can't really hear as I'm leaving the bathroom. Not that I want to know what she's saying, since it's probably not going to be nice. Outside, I lean against the wall in the corridor and wait for her.

Finally, after nearly ten minutes, the bathroom door

opens, and she walks out.

"Come on," she says, tossing a glance in my direction before turning and striding off.

I have to run to catch up to her, and we walk in silence. The entire time I'm trying to watch the way her arms swing, turning in slightly, and the way she holds her head, her neck stretched. It's like she's had lessons in walking correctly.

"Stop staring at me." Tilly comes to an abrupt halt and glares at me.

I take a step backward and focus on the floor.

"S-s-s-orry. Z-zac said…"

"I don't care what Zac said. Just give it a rest. I'm not the main attraction in a circus." She frowns. "Despite what the media would have you believe," she adds, her voice sounding flat.

I glance up and see a strange, almost despondent, expression on her face, which hardens as soon as she notices me looking.

"Sorry," I repeat. "What do you want to do?"

"I need to go over some moves. The last girl was next to useless."

That surprises me, seeing as the original stunt double was a professional. The producers wouldn't have taken her on if she couldn't do the job. Unless it's just Tilly being Tilly. Whatever. It's sort of a relief, because her having been awesome in Tilly's mind would have added even more pressure.

"Okay," I say, following her.

We take the stairs to the next level, to a part of the building I haven't been to before. At the end of the corridor there are a set of double doors, which Tilly pushes open, taking us into a practice room. The back wall is mirrored, and there are practice bars all around the other walls.

"Mats are over there," Tilly says, pointing to where there are a few standing in the corner. "And they call this place a movie studio," she adds, scanning the room. "Just look at it."

I don't reply, just run to the corner, pick up a mat, and bring it over, unrolling it and laying it on the floor. Then I take off my shoes and stand in the middle. Tilly does the same. I'm not sure exactly what she wants to know. Whether it's just basic stuff, like how to stand, or what.

"Stand with your feet apart and your knees slightly bent." *Yay, no stutter.*

"I know that," Tilly snaps, rolling her eyes toward the ceiling. "I'm not a total idiot."

This whole situation is just weird. Here I am, facing someone I've worshipped for most of my life, and instead of it being the best time ever, it's turning into a nightmare. I know on screen it's all acting. But how can she be so totally different from the characters she plays and yet so convincing? It's crazy.

"S-s-sorry." *Crap.*

"Show me how to kick. The roundabout kick."

A laugh escapes my lips, and my hand shoots up to cover my mouth.

"What's so funny?" Tilly demands, her eyes narrow.

"Nothing. It's called the roundhouse kick." I chew on my bottom lip. And wait for snarky comment. Except it doesn't come.

"Show me." Tilly stands opposite me, in the correct starting position, concentration etched across her perfect, porcelain-skinned face.

I've been training juniors for a while, so I decide to treat it like that. I'm not facing a Hollywood star. She's just someone who wants to learn about kickboxing. And if she wants to get it right, she needs to do as I say. I shake out my arms and stand with my legs slightly apart and bent.

"The roundhouse is a turning kick. Lift your knee up and out, like this." I show her, maintaining the first position. "And then twist your hip toward your target and flick your upper shin out." I kick out into the air. "You try. Aim at my leg."

Tilly lifts her knee, but her hips aren't flexible, and she misses me by miles.

"Like this." I face her, twist, and kick out at the same time she moves slightly forward, and I catch her on the thigh.

"Ouch," Tilly cries, leaning over and rubbing her leg.

"I'm so sorry. Are you okay?" Why the hell wasn't I

more careful? She's gonna really have it in for me now.

"I'm fine," Tilly says waving her arm dismissively. "Just go."

I do as she says, but not before catching the grimace on her face out the corner of my eye.

Just when I was starting to feel a little more confident in front of her.

Chapter Five

"Ouch," I whimper.

"Well, keep still. I told you, this is delicate work," Mel, our makeup girl (or should I say sadist), snaps.

What I want to know is why no one's ever seen fit to tell me we have hairs on our ears? Okay, it might not be a topic of everyday conversation, but you'd have thought someone would've mentioned it. I had no idea, having never seen the hairs on mine, which is hardly surprising since they're so fine you'd need a magnifying glass to notice them. Knowing would've prepared me for the excruciating pain Mel is putting me through each time she adjusts my fairy ears. Then again, if I had known, it would've given me something extra to worry about.

I haven't seen Tilly since our kickboxing lesson. Is

it naïve to wonder if, now that I helped her, she doesn't totally hate me? I hope she's recovered from the kick, though. It wasn't that hard—the same light-contact kick I would use with new junior kickboxing students sparring for the first time—so I'm sure she'll be okay.

Finally, or should that be frighteningly, I'm going to be doing some real, filmed stand-in work for Tilly. We're on location in the Hills, and it's taking hours to get me ready. I've been in the make-up trailer since five in the morning, and I'm telling you, if I don't get out of this chair soon, I'll pee my pants.

As for what they've done to my broken nose, it's incredible. Mel's assistant has been working on me for a long time, including adding silicone to the sides—to flatten it, she said, and give it the appearance of being smaller. Well, I'm all for that, but it was a bit worrying when she covered half my face with something that looked remarkably like the filler Dad uses at home to fix holes in the wall. And now my face feels all stiff. I wonder if this is what Botox is like. But I can't deny that the end result is perfect.

"Sorry, Mel."

"Abi. This is the *real* side of movie work. Lots of hanging around waiting to be called on set. Hours in make-up. Nothing like people imagine. So if you want to make a career of this, I suggest you get used to it. And…" she narrows her eyes slightly. "Learn to keep still."

A career of it? She'd never believe me if I told her that, up until a few weeks ago, a career in the movies was the furthest thing from my dreams as was possible. Now? It's anyone's guess.

"Sorry, Mel."

"Don't keep saying sorry. If you want to survive here, you've got to stand up for yourself and not keep apologizing for everything. No one will respect you for it." She gives my shoulder a gentle squeeze. "You're a good kid. Remember that. And take no notice of anything Tilly says."

That's easy for her to say. It will be hard not to take notice of Tilly. And what's with the *stand up for yourself* bit? Doesn't she know I get enough of that talk when I'm at home or with Liv and Matt? What I'm doing now, actually being a stunt double, is me standing on my own two feet and pushing myself further than I've ever been before, and that includes the kickboxing.

"I'll try," I say, trying to stop the grimace from showing on my face as yet another ear hair is pulled.

Mel turns her head. "Bring over the wig," she calls to her assistant.

She swings around the chair I'm sitting in so I can no longer see my reflection, and then takes hold of a wig that is very long and very dark, almost black, and a replica of the one Tilly has been wearing in her scenes. She stretches out the rubbery head-cap. While she's pulling it over my head, she accidentally catches my scalp with her nail, which hurts big-time, but I bite on my bottom lip to keep from calling out, determined to keep my game face on.

In my peripheral vision, I notice Mel's assistant staring at me. Actually, more than staring, gaping—her eyes are wide and her mouth is open.

What's wrong? I hope my nose hasn't slipped. Or the ears. Just the thought of having to have them reapplied today is causing me to break out in hives. Tomorrow is soon enough to experience this process again.

Mel must also catch sight of her staring, because she glares at her. "Call wardrobe and say Abi's on her way, then go to the supplies cupboard and stock up."

"Okay," Mel says, changing the subject. "Let's get you to wardrobe. You know where it is?" She takes hold of my arm and helps me off the chair, marching me toward the door. So I don't even get chance to see what I look like.

"Yes. But I'm just going to go to the bathroom and grab a quick breakfast, if that's okay?"

"Okay? Of course it's not okay. For goodness sake. Didn't you listen to anything I said? This isn't a playground. We're on a tight schedule. You have to be on set by eight. Which is in precisely..." She glances down at her watch. "Which is in precisely twenty minutes. Go to the bathroom, if you must, then get your butt over to wardrobe. Breakfast can wait." She shakes her head then turns on her heel and walks toward the sink.

I pull out a half-eaten chocolate bar from my bag and shove it down while half walking and half jogging to the bathroom. I go as quickly as I can, cursing the faded spot on the wall where a mirror used to hang over the sink, then high-tail it to wardrobe.

"I don't have much time. I'm due on set soon," I say.

Fran from wardrobe waves her hand dismissively. "Don't worry. They're bound to be running late."

Fran's so relaxed compared to Mel, but I'll stick with what Mel says, just be sure. I don't want to get a reputation for being a bad worker.

"Yes, but I don't want to risk it."

Fran strides over to one of the rails, which is crammed full of costumes, and takes the one hanging on the end. She pulls off the cover to reveal not *just* a dress, but a freakin' gorgeous dress with a pale blue bodice, tiny diamond drops around the neckline, and a long handkerchief skirt in a deep midnight blue. It has to be the most amazing outfit ever—and this coming from someone who'd rather wear jeans than anything showing legs any day of the week.

"What do you think? Fit for a fairy princess?" She takes hold of the skirt at the bottom and stretches it out so the intricate pattern on the lace is visible.

"I've never seen anything like it before," I gasp.

"You won't," Fran replies, a smile tugging at her lips. "I made it especially for the movie."

"Wow. I love it."

"It wasn't easy, though." Fran shakes her head. "I wanted to capture the essence of the myth without compromising the contemporary feel. Of course, you've got to be able to do all the action scenes, so you need plenty of leg room."

"What happens if the costumes get damaged?"

"We'll take the replacement cost out of your wages, so you best make sure you don't ruin it." She gives me a threatening glare over the rims of her boxy black glasses, snapping her gum in my direction.

That's all I need. Instead of them paying me, I could end up owing them money by the end of the shoot. "I-I-I won't. I mean, I'll try not to, but, you know, what I have to do... it isn't easy and..."

"Abi. Abi. Stop. I was kidding." She can't finish because she's giggling so much.

"Oh. I didn't realize. I thought you meant it." I start to laugh and hope she can't tell it's forced. Because inside I'm not really laughing. I'm just feeling stupid.

"You need to lighten up and not take everything so seriously. Or you'll drive yourself crazy."

"Sorry."

"Accidents happen. We expect them to. We've got four of these dresses all identical to each other. Two for you and two for Tilly. Which means if one gets damaged you can wear the other one while we make repairs. Come on, let's get this on, since you don't want to be late." She hands me the dress. "Don't forget this." She holds out a skin-tone, strapless, padded bra.

"Thanks."

"It fits like a normal bra, only it's got silicone inserts to give you curves like Tilly. Call me when you've got it on so I can adjust it to the correct shape."

"Okay."

After Fran adjusts the bra, which is so embarrassing since it pretty much involves her getting to second base several times over, I pull on the dress. It fastens at the front with tiny, dark blue pearl buttons that are so small it takes me forever to do them. I'm going to be really late, I know it.

"Abi, hurry up. Do you need help?" Even Fran is sounding anxious now, which starts my heart racing.

"I'm coming." I quickly slip on the matching blue flats Fran gave me and step out into the room and walk towards her. She holds her hand up to her mouth.

"Abi, look at you. Just look at you." Her eyes are wide and sparkly, unless it's a magnifying trick of her reading glasses, as she wheels a mirror across the floor and pushes it in front of me.

My heart's thumping loudly in my ears. This is what I've been waiting to see all morning.

Oh. My. God.

My eyes wide, I step gingerly toward the mirror until I'm only an arm's length away and stare. This is so weird, it's screwing with my head. How can it be? That reflection isn't me. Definitely not me.

It's Tilly.

I am Tilly.

Even down to the nose, which I keep going on about, it's just like…well, just like hers. I now have a perfectly shaped nose, thanks to the silicone prosthetic. I've wanted a perfect nose since forever, and now I have one.

It's insane.

"Well?" Fran's excited voice reminds me I'm not alone. "What do you think?"

"I have no words." And I don't.

Never in a million years did I imagine they'd be able to make me look like Tilly. It's just crazy. I'd love to get out my phone and take a selfie, but there isn't time and Fran might not approve.

"You better get going," she reminds me as she ushers me out the door.

It's quite a hike to the set from the wardrobe trailer, so it's another five minutes before I get there, by which time the excitement has got my heart pounding like crazy against my ribcage. I can't wait to see what Vince and the others say when they see me.

Zac looks up when I approach, then almost immediately breaks out into a huge smile. He must be on something. Zac doesn't do smiling. At least not in my direction. Not that he's rude. Most of the time, he acts like I don't exist. That I'm invisible. Which I guess I am to him. All he cares about is getting the shot in the can as quickly as possible.

He strides over to me like a man on a mission.

"Tilly, daaaarling," he leans forward, rests his hands very gently on my shoulders and air kisses me on both cheeks. True European style. "I don't need you yet. Not until later this morning." He steps back and smiles. Again.

"It's Abi," I say, my voice barely above a whisper, trying to suppress a giggle, because for him to think I'm Tilly is ridiculous. Though I can't help but notice that I didn't stutter. Is it because I'm so comfortable around Zac now, or is it because I'm dressed as Tilly? Either way, I like it.

He lifts his shades and rests them on top of his head, then looks back at me and shakes his head. "Well, I'll be damned. You're a dead ringer for Tilly. I could always see a resemblance in your build and the way you walk, but this. And your nose... Mel's certainly outdone herself."

I don't believe it. He's actually being nice. Not sure I'm buying the resemblance between me and Tilly *before* this make-over, unless I'm not seeing something others are, since he isn't the first person to say so. Whatever. I don't care. The main thing is that now that they've transformed me, he's pleased.

. . .

I'm leaning against the tree at the entrance waiting for Matt to arrive to give me a ride home. I persuaded Mel to let me stay in full wig and make up until he gets here so I can fool him into thinking I'm Tilly. Especially as I'm sure he has a crush on her. Maybe that's why he's always offering to pick me up. He wants to bump into her. Well, today he will. Sort of. I can't stop laughing to myself. I can just imagine his face when finds out it's really me.

After a few minutes, Matt's car turns into the parking lot, and without staring over there directly, I watch as he jumps out of the car and strides toward the entrance. As he gets within a few yards of me, I start walking in his direction and keep looking ahead, acting like I don't know who he is.

"Hey," Matt says as I walk right past him. I don't turn around just keep on walking. "Hey," he repeats.

I slowly turn my head around and look at him from under my lashes, in the same way I've seen Tilly do on screen hundreds of times. It takes me all of my self-control not to break down and give myself away. "Yes?" I say in my best Tilly East-Coast accent.

He frowns. "Abi, what are you doing?"

My jaw drops, but I quickly pull myself together. "Excuse me? Do I know you?" I say, except this time my accent slips slightly.

"I think you do, *Abi.*" His eyes always sparkle when he teases me. And that's what they're doing now.

"I'm not Abi. I'm Tilly." I start to giggle, the effect now completely ruined.

So much for fooling him. But I don't get it. Everyone says I'm identical to Tilly. I even fooled Zac. So how on earth did he know that it's me under all this disguise?

He arches an eyebrow. "Nice try. But no cigar. I'll always know you, no matter how much crap you have on your face."

Chapter Six

"Ready?" Vince yells, as he revs the motorcycle engine.

"Ready," I shout in his ear, keeping my face turned into his neck so I don't choke on the gas fumes.

We're attempting, for about the twentieth time, the scene on the bridge where Hui and Princess Wairere escape her tribe, and he takes her back to his, where his father is chief.

Zac's instructions are for me to look exhilarated while we ride across the bridge at breakneck speed, which is easier said than done.

Vince nods, which is the signal to show we're okay to start.

"Action," shouts Zac.

I sit up, keeping my neck straight, plaster on a fake

excited look (which isn't too difficult, seeing as facial expressions for exhilaration and scared are closely related), tighten my grip around Vince's waist with my extremely sweaty hands, and start to pray.

It only takes a few seconds before we get to the bridge, and as we hit the wooden planks and the bike wobbles, I can't stop my eyes from glancing down into the ravine.

Crap, if we fall, we'll die. How can it be otherwise when we're not wearing helmets or any other protection?

"Cut," Zac shouts.

"Abi," Zac growls, when he gets within hearing distance. "Do you know what exhilarated means?" I nod. "Then why do you insist on looking like a scared rabbit all the time?"

"I'm sorry," I mumble. "It's just the…"

"Don't give me your excuses. Just get it right. We have little enough time as it is, without you delaying us even more."

My whole body tenses. It's easy for him to say *just get it right*. Doesn't he get that I'm trying my hardest? It's like being back at school when teachers would lose their patience and finish off my sentences for me. Well, he should try looking exhilarated when his life flashes before his eyes. And FYI, hollering isn't gonna help. This is all new stuff to me. And maybe he should remember that I'm way better now than when we first started. And

I'll be even better soon. That's a promise.

"I'll do it." Tilly says walking up to Zac. She heaves an exasperated sigh and flips her hair over her shoulder in that trademark way she has. It used to seem such a cute gesture. Now it just makes me want to disappear into a hole in the ground.

"No, Tilly," Zac says. "It's too dangerous. We've had this discussion before. You're too valuable. We can't risk it."

Tilly wants to do her own stunts? Who knew? She's never given any hint of that so far, apart from getting me to show her some moves. Her coordination was only average, and that's putting it nicely. Good to know she's valuable and I'm not. I know that's the life of a stunt double, but it's not nice to hear someone put it into words.

"Then do something." She gestures in my direction, and I feel the color shoot up my cheeks.

"Why don't you spend a few minutes going over the scene with Abi and show her some moves and facial expressions?" Zac suggests, although his suggestion doesn't seem open for discussion. "Back in twenty," he calls to everyone.

"I suppose so." Tilly sighs, clearly not happy with Zac's idea. "Come on," she says to me before heading toward the trees that lead to the river.

I hurry to catch up. "Th-th-anks," I say when I get close to her, but she doesn't reply, just keeps walking until we get to a small clearing in the trees.

"Right. Just watch," Tilly says. "It's not rocket science. Even for you."

"That's easy for you to say," I reply, actually getting angry enough that I don't stutter. I don't get her. She's acting like I didn't help her the other day. But if I can help her, then she should be nice about helping me. In my world, that's how it works. "You've been acting your whole life. You're a star. I'm a kickboxer."

Something about my words seems to penetrate her icy exterior. Her face softens for just a moment as she brushes the long, black wig back from her perfect cheekbones. "Seriously, it's really not that hard. Let me show you something my first acting coach taught me…"

• • •

"Good work," Zac shouts. "Everyone meet back here after lunch."

Yay! After the twenty-fifth take, Zac is *finally* satisfied. I feel like punching the air, but that isn't cool. So I just act like it's nothing. After Tilly's demonstration, which she actually managed to make helpful and deliver in a patient tone once she got going, everything seemed to fall into place. For all her faults, there's no denying she's talented.

"Yo, Tilly. Good job," Nathan says, as he walks past.

Nathan has never said anything about my work

before. He's Tilly's leading man and so nice. And gay, much to Liv's disappointment. I'd never heard of him, but she remembers him from some obscure children's TV show on cable about ten years ago.

"Thanks...but it's Abi," I mutter, more to myself than anyone else as Nathan is way out of earshot.

"Abi. Or should I say Tilly? You were smoking." Vince rests his arm across my shoulder and grins. "I wonder what Tilly will say when she sees your performance on screen."

"Something nice I hope, seeing as she helped me," I say.

"Wonder no more. I was watching." The sound of Tilly's voice from behind makes me jump.

I spin on my heel until I'm facing her. "H-h-h-hi, T-T-Tilly." I inwardly squirm under her scrutiny. And a flush creeps slowly up my face. Typical. Would it really hurt if just once I could play it cool?

A smirk crosses her face. Yeah, well, stuttering might be funny to Tilly, but it's not to me.

"Just don't get any ideas," she says, a teasing grin on her face. Although, am I the only one who notices how her normally big brown eyes have narrowed to tiny slits? Or that there's a definite smell of whiskey on her breath that wasn't there earlier? "There's only one Tilly Watson. Got it?" I nod. She turns, takes a couple of steps then glances back at me from over her shoulder. "You did well. Eventually."

Excuse me. Either I'm dreaming, or Tilly just complimented me on my stunt work. "I don't believe it," I say to no one in particular.

"Believe it," says Vince. "You've just been Tilly'd. She knocks you down, then gives you a pat on the back to show you no hard feelings. Because whatever she says, she wants you to love her. She *needs* you to love her. To idolize her, even, like all her fans."

Yeah, well she's not going the right way about it. At least, not with me.

"Why?" I frown.

"Insecurity," Vince replies.

"And on what planet does someone like Tilly feel insecure around someone like me?"

"You're good at what you do, and she sees you as a threat," he says, shrugging.

Me a threat. That's a joke. The only time I'm a threat to anyone is when I'm on the mat kickboxing.

"I'm not a threat. It's the other way round. If I upset Tilly, then she could get me kicked out. Zac's hardly going to choose me over her, is he?"

"Abi," Vince says in an exaggerated impression of Zac's I'm-trying-to-be-patient voice. "Who's running the show?"

"Zac."

"And does Zac strike you as someone who can be easily manipulated?"

"Okay, okay. I get it. But, it's easy for you to say."

"Just go with the flow," Vince says. "She's under contract, too. And her life isn't as perfect as people think. She's under a lot of pressure."

"Really? I would have said her life was pretty near perfect. Doing a job most girls would kill for. Fame. Money. Can do anything she wants. How bad can that be?"

"Don't get sucked in by the myth of Hollywood glitz and glamour. I'm not saying that she doesn't enjoy being a star. Just that it's not all it's cracked up to be. Why do you think she has a problem with alcohol?" Vince shakes his head.

"I guess. But it's hard to cut her some slack when she has so much attitude." Which makes me sound like a petty child.

"I'm not asking you to," Vince says. "All I'm saying is try and remember that she doesn't have it easy a lot of the time."

Chapter Seven

"I want ten jumping jacks and then run in place until I tell you to stop," I say to a group of juniors who are standing in front of me, eagerly waiting to start.

When Bill called, asking if I could train the juniors for him since he'd been let down by one of the other trainers, I said yes right away. As much as I love working on the movie, the thought of coming back to the dojo excited me, particularly since I would see some friendly faces and be able to tell them what I've been doing. Except, when I went to see Bill, all he did was wave and continue shuffling papers on his desk. You'd think he'd show a little more interest seeing as he was the one to start the whole thing.

While the juniors are warming up, I scan the dojo

and out the corner of my eye notice Matt walking around the edge. My heart does a quick flip. He looks as gorgeous as ever. He doesn't see me immediately, but when he does, his face lights up. I beckon for him to come over, and he heads in my direction.

"Hey," he says when he reaches me. "You didn't say you'd be here today." He gives me a hug and ruffles my hair.

"I wanted to surprise you," I say, pulling away from him and smoothing down my hair. He knows the trouble I have with my hair because it's so fine and thinks it's funny to mess with it. I pretend it bothers me more than it does. "Bill's asked me to help out with the juniors. I thought we could go out for lunch after. My treat. Unless you have other plans." I arch an eyebrow, knowing full well that if I'm offering lunch, there's no way he'll refuse.

"I've got to go to the store for groceries for Mom, but that can wait until later. Especially if *you're* paying, I'm not missing out on that." He ducks out of the way of my pretend swipe around his head. "Actually, if I give you Mom's list, you could go for me since my class ends after yours. Then we won't have to rush lunch," Matt says, shooting me a lopsided grin that's guaranteed to get me to agree. He sure knows how to play me—all girls, actually. Not that I mind. It's just how it is.

"Okay, I guess. But you owe me one," I say. Actually, he owes me more than one, the number of times I've done his chores for him.

"You got it," he says, winking.

"Cool. See you later."

"By the way, if you don't want Bill on your back, then you need to get your class in line," he says, pointing behind me.

I turn and notice a couple of the juniors pushing each other. Typical. Can't they even behave for one minute? And now I look bad.

"Well, he should be grateful that I could help him out, considering how busy I am."

"Listen to Miss Fancy-Pants Movie Star." Matt looks toward the ceiling and shakes his head.

"Shut up. You know I'm not like that. But there's no harm in a bit of appreciation, is there?" On set, the stunt coordinators are always saying how well I'm doing. Well, maybe not always, but a lot. And here? Well, there's certainly no fear of compliment overload, that's for sure.

"Of course not. You know we *really, really, really* appreciate you," Matt teases.

"Go away," I say giving him a gentle push. "I'll see you after class."

I jog back to the juniors. "Okay, listen up. In pairs I want to see one of you kick and the other block. Do that ten times and then swap over. Anyone misbehaving has Bill to answer to."

. . .

After the juniors finish, I go to the locker room to shower. I pull on my street clothes and, instead of doing Matt's grocery shopping, decide to go and watch the senior class—we can shop later after lunch when there's more time. Matt won't mind.

Leaning against the wall gives me a good view of Matt sparring with one of the other guys. He lands a strong roundhouse kick to the chest, then blocks. Then he does an effective front kick. The other guy is on the defensive, mainly blocking, and doesn't seem to notice the gap that Matt keeps leaving when using his left arm. I'm the only girl who's allowed to work with Matt, since I'm the only one so far who's made it into the advanced ranks like he has. Maybe that's why I can see the gaps, because we fight so often. He knows all of my weak spots, too.

Bill calling the end of class distracts me from my thoughts, and I wander to the main entrance to wait for Matt. After ten minutes, I see him walking toward me, his hair damp and clinging to his face.

"Ready?" he asks.

"Yep. Should we go to the Fountain?"

The Fountain's our second favorite place to go. It's close, and they do the most amazing fruit smoothies.

"Sounds good to me," Matt says. "I'm so hungry I could eat the entire menu."

While we're walking, he talks non-stop about the

latest *Grand Theft Auto*. He's a total gamer and is always trying to get me and Liv to play. It's fun for half an hour, but after that I get bored. I really don't get how people can pull gaming all-nighters.

When we get to the café, we sit down and wait for someone to take our order.

"Don't you want to know how the movie is going?" I'm feeling a little miffed that he hasn't even bothered to ask. Especially as I haven't seen him for a while. You'd think he'd show some interest. It's not like it's something people do every day of their lives.

"I figured you'd tell me eventually. You usually do." He shrugs.

What does he mean by that? It's not like I go on and on about the movie set. At least I don't think I do. Liv hasn't mentioned it. She can't get enough of it. She always wants to know everything that goes on. All we've ever known before is what we've read in the magazines or online. Now I'm getting everything firsthand. It's a real eye-opener.

"Well, I won't if you're not interested." I scowl at him.

"Now look who's having a movie star tantrum," he says arching a brow.

"I'm not." I fold my arms tightly across my chest, but can't stay mad for long. He's right. I am acting no better than Tilly and her tantrums. "Okay, I'll tell you, whether you want to hear or not."

Chapter Eight

"Emotion, Tilly. Emotion." The frustrated look on Zac's face belies the tolerant tone in his voice.

He's definitely losing it with her. Who can blame him? Judging by the state Tilly came in this morning, he'll get more emotion from the tree she's leaning against. This is take fifteen, and each one has been as bad as the next. It's like she's not trying. It's written all over her face. Every time Zac calls action, she gives an extremely loud sigh and deliberately screws it up. Why? What the hell does she hope to gain by it?

I was in make-up when she arrived earlier, at about eight, and I didn't recognize her right away because she looked so rough. Her hair was matted. She had black rings under her eyes, which were dull and lifeless. I don't think she'd showered because there was a definite whiff of stale sweat in the air. It was disgusting. Lucky for the rest of us, Mel made her go and wash.

And I overheard Mel say that she overheard Nathan say that the hotel's night manager was moaning to the day manager about the noise coming from Tilly's suite last night. I wonder who she was with and what they were doing? You'd think she'd try to be more discreet. Not that it's any of my business, even if I can't wait to tell Liv who, like me, will be dying to know everything that happened.

"You try being emotional with a script like this." Tilly folds her arms and glares at Zac like a petulant child. She's treading on dangerous ground if you ask me.

Zac strides toward her, visibly relaxing his facial muscles on his way. "You're the best, Tilly. You can do it. Come on, do it for me. Let's wrap this scene up," he says when he's standing in front of her. He turns away from Tilly, the expression on his face unreadable, and faces the crew. "Okay, guys. Close up on Tilly, show her emotion at seeing Hui alive, then camera left to shoot Abi from behind as she runs with Vince and jumps on the back of the motorcycle."

What is it with this movie that I seem to spend so much time jumping onto the back of a motorcycle? I don't see why they can't keep using the same shot each time. Who's going to know? Okay, I guess that's not the attitude, and without all these shots I'd be hanging around doing not a lot, but even so.

"Make sure you shoot from the waist up. I don't want my fans thinking I have a b-b-b-butt the size of an elephant," Tilly growls.

Suddenly, all eyes are on me, and I just know my face is crimson. When will she stop with the mockery? I won't let her see I'm upset, though, because she'll only be worse. Not that anyone is going to say anything to her about it.

She's the star.

What's wrong with my butt, anyway? It's not that big, and everyone says Tilly and I are the same size. Plus now I have my fake boobs, which makes me a lot more curvy and in proportion than before.

"Ignore her," says Vince cutting into my thoughts. "She's not having a good day. And by the way, your butt is fine." He casts a glance at my ass and nods.

You know, when Vince is made up to look like Nathan, he's quite cute, with his dark, close-cropped curls and big brown eyes. Not that I have the hots for him in that way. He's just a great guy to hang out with. I prefer the less chiseled and more ruffled look, like… like… No, I'm not going down that path. Matt's just a friend.

"Thanks. I just don't get why she has to be like this when she has such an amazing life."

Even if what Vince says about being a star—about how it's not all it's hyped up to be—is true, there are still millions of girls in this world who would give everything to have what Tilly has, and she should stop for a moment and think about that. I know that if the positions were reversed and I was the movie star, then I'd be nice to everyone and I'd be grateful for everything I had.

Even just doing this gig I'm pretty grateful, because it's more than most girls my age would ever get to do.

"It might seem amazing to you, but her career is close to the edge. No one will employ her. This low-budget movie is her last chance," Vince says, folding his arms across his chest and leaning against the tree.

"You're kidding. Why, when her movies are so successful? I don't get it."

"Because she's so hard to manage, and directors are getting sick of having to deal with it. Every time she pulls a diva routine, it costs the studio money. The producers get pissed since they have to pay all of the crew overtime because movies are behind schedule. She's not as bankable as she used to be, and if she's not bringing in the money she's costing the studio…"

"I had no idea." I shake my head.

So the investors really are taking a huge risk. Scary for them if everything depends on Tilly pulling it off. Maybe that's why they had to hire a total unknown like me. If Tilly screws up, they stand to lose a lot of money, so they have to keep costs down in other areas where they can. I sort of feel sorry for her.

"No, they—"

"Action," says Zac, cutting dead my conversation with Vince.

We both turn and look at Tilly.

"Hui. You're here. They told me you were dead." As Tilly clings to Nathan, tears stream down her face. Finally, we get to see the Tilly magic. It's incredible that with so few words she can give the most spell-binding, heart-wrenching performance. It even brings tears to my eyes. It's so amazing how she can turn it on for the camera, when she wants to. Yet for me, every time I speak it's a monumental effort, requiring absolute concentration.

Her attitude aside, I could learn a lot from Tilly.

. . .

"Cut and hold," yells Zac. "Good work everyone. Abi, you were spot on. And Tilly, you should be more like Abi. Have an early night, get plenty of rest, and leave the liquor alone."

Whoa! I can't believe he just said that. I'm desperate to take a look at Tilly's face to see how she's taking it, except I can't since when Zac says hold, it means we're not allowed to move until the cameraman says so. He has to check that everything's okay and that the scene's in the can and, if it isn't, we have to go over it again. So it's important for continuity we stay where we are. Which, for me, is sitting behind Vince on the motorcycle, looking behind as we've managed to escape from our pursuers. A few minutes later, we get the all clear, and I swing my leg around, get off, and head toward the resting tent. My work for the morning is done.

"Hey, you. Abi." I glance up and see Tilly heading in my direction. And she doesn't look like she's in a good mood.

"Yes?"

"I know what you're doing; don't think I don't," she says in a harsh voice that's barely above a whisper but still sends a shiver down my spine.

Not that I have a clue what's she's talking about.

"Sorry?"

"Trying to make me look bad in front of Zac."

This has got to be a bad dream. Since when have I ever done anything to make Tilly look bad? I know Zac said she should be more like me, but he didn't mean it. Not really.

"I'm n-not doing anything. I wouldn't do that to you."

"I'm n-n-n-not doing anything," Tilly says, imitating me so well it's like talking to myself. "Don't give me that crap." She narrows her eyes. *"Yes, Zac. No Zac. How do you want me to do this, Zac? Is that all right, Zac. Let me kiss your butt, Zac."*

Why doesn't she just shut the hell up and leave me alone? So what if I'm doing as I'm told? I don't know how much more I can take of her going off on me like this. At least, not without landing a kick right where it hurts. Well, in my dreams that's what I'd do.

"I just wanted to get it right. For the movie. I wasn't trying to get you in trouble." My voice starts to quiver, and it takes all my resolve to pull it back in. There's no way I'm going to lose it in front of her, because she'll just love that.

"Tilly." Fraser's call distracts her, and she turns from me.

"What?"

"Zac wants to speak to you about the next scene."

"Now what does he want? We went over all this yesterday." She looks back at me and rolls her eyes to the sky. "That man. I'll tell you, he must be the worst director I've worked with."

She lets out a long groan then slowly walks back towards the main set area, slouching and dragging her feet all the way.

I watch until she's out of sight, conscious only of my heart pounding mercilessly against my ribcage. I just don't get it. I'm trying to do a good job for *her* movie. I'd be happy if she'd just treat me consistently, instead of one day being okay and the next being awful.

I can't go wait in the resting tent. Not when everyone else is there, because they'll want to talk, and now I'm not up to that. I just need to be by myself, to think. I'll go sit by the river. There's no filming there today, so I should be undisturbed.

The river is a few minutes' walk away, and on the way I can't help but notice the peace and quiet. Well, not peace and quiet as in total silence, but no voices or motorcycles— just the sound of the birds.

When I get there, I'm just about to sit on the ground at the water's edge when, luckily, I remember my dress. If I get it dirty, Fran will go mad because I ripped the other one on Wednesday, all down the back, and it might not have been repaired yet.

Instead, I sit on a large rock and wrap my arms around my knees. I rest my chin on them and draw in a lungful of fresh air.

I'm so sick of Tilly treating me like her whipping girl, I could scream. I know when Danny offered me the role I was unsure, but I hoped, deep down, that it would be a great experience. I mean, look how well kickboxing worked out. I didn't want to do that either, but ended up discovering something I was completely passionate about.

Since I got this role because of kickboxing, it should work out, right?

Wrong.

How much of a loser would they think I am if I say I don't want to do the job anymore? The way I'm feeling today, I'd really like to. But would I dare? Would I be allowed to, seeing as I signed a contract? I wonder if it says anything about leaving. What if I had to give back all the money I've earned so far? I've already spent some on Christmas presents and on an adorable pair of jeans.

I strum my fingers on my leg and mentally give myself a shake. I'm being so pathetic, thinking of giving up at the first hurdle. Working on a movie set is just like being at the dojo. We're a team. We look out for each other; well, some more than others. Even so, I've got to stick at it. I actually need to be more like Tilly and grow a backbone. She doesn't let anyone push her around. I'm not saying I want to be exactly like her, just that there are some things I could take from her.

A rustling noise from behind brings me back to the present. I jerk my head around and quickly scan my surroundings, but there's nothing there.

I hear the noise again, only this time it's coming from my left. Yikes. The hairs on the back of my neck stand at attention, and my arms have goose bumps running down them. I jump up from the rock and quickly look from side to side but see nothing. Is it an animal? Or a person? Whatever, something's not right. Crap. What should I do? It might be a stalker. You read all sorts of things about stalkers and their obsession with movie stars and how they find their way into the star's bedroom and…

"Gotcha," a male voice whispers in my ear at the same time covering my eyes with his hand.

I open my mouth, but before any sound comes out, he spins my body around and my jaw drops as I glimpse a guy so cute he should be illegal. He kisses me firmly on the lips.

A butterfly sensation shoots through my stomach in the split second between wanting to lose myself in his kiss, which is totally crazy, and panic.

Luckily, reality takes hold, and I know I need to think of something quick, before he does something horrific to me. No one just kisses a stranger like this without having creepy motives. So, using as much force as I can muster, I put my hands on his shoulders and push him away, while at the same time lifting my leg and aiming a front kick at his groin, which doesn't quite connect because of the uneven surface. I lose my balance and fall over backward, landing on my butt.

Pain shoots through my tailbone, but there's no time to nurse my wounds. I scramble to my feet and race towards the trees.

"Tilly," he calls. "What are you doing? It's me. Stop."

Chapter Nine

Me? What does he mean me? Who's me?

I slow down to practically walking pace and glance over my shoulder. He's standing there, hands on hips, staring in my direction. There's something really familiar about him, but I can't think what. Come to think of it, he did call me Tilly. He thinks I'm Tilly. He kissed me thinking I was Tilly.

"I thought you'd be happy to see me," he calls out. "And not trying to get as far away from me as possible."

I can't just disappear. Not now. He deserves an explanation. I begin to walk back to where he's standing.

"S-s-sorry," I say, when I get within a couple of feet of him. "I'm..."

"Not. Tilly," he says deliberately, his jaw dropping

in the process. "I'm *so* sorry. I shouldn't have done that. From behind, you look just like her. The front, too. It's ridiculous, I'm sorry."

Could he be any nicer, apologizing like that to me? How lucky is Tilly having him as her boyfriend?

"I-I'm Abi. Tilly's double."

"The likeness is uncanny. I'd never have known if it wasn't for your st...umm... voice."

Yeah, I get it. My stutter. How embarrassing. But at least he corrected himself and didn't actually say it. That's more than a lot of people have done in the past.

"Oh." I force my hands to remain by my side and not fly up to my cheeks which are radiating heat.

"Tilly's mentioned you."

"Oh." That's just great. Now Tilly's gossiping about me.

"Don't look so worried. She hasn't said anything awful, like she thinks you're an axe-murderer. Just that you're her double and doing a good job." A lazy smile crosses his face, and my heart skips a beat.

Is he serious? Tilly's praising me to... to...whoever he is. Maybe I misjudged her. Or maybe I don't figure enough in her life for her to think about me away from the set.

"Oh."

"*Oh*. Is that the full extent of your vocabulary?" He laughs, and two little dimples appear in his cheeks. "I'm Jon, by the way, Tilly's boyfriend." He frowns ever so slightly. "Long distance, most of the time." His gorgeous blue eyes cloud over and look all wistful, and the dimples disappear.

Then it clicks. Jon Redcliffe. How could I have not recognized him sooner? Though, in my defense, he's just started breaking out in Hollywood, and in his last movie he was covered in alien goo for most of it.

I remember seeing pictures of him with Tilly on People.com and Radar Online, but he's much cuter in real life. I love the way his dark hair curls around his ears. And his eyes are so blue it's like they're tinted contacts. He's shorter than I thought he'd be, but that's okay—he's still taller than me. His accent is to die for, British with a hint of American on some words. Of course he's with Tilly, and I'd never have a chance with someone like him. Guys that hot don't give me a second look. Even if I am interested. Which I'm not.

Well, I could be. Who wouldn't if the chance arose?

I can't wait to tell Liv about him.

"Oh." *Abi. Get a grip.* "I-I mean, that's a shame. I suppose it must be hard to get away from work when she's on the other side of the world."

"We're used to it. It's okay if we're working on the same movie."

"Are you going to be working on our movie then?"

"No. I'm between jobs at the moment. Thought I'd fly out to surprise Tilly. I arrived last night."

So, now we know what she was doing all night. My

head's full of images of him and Tilly in her hotel room, making enough noise to alert the staff and set off the local gossip chain, and my face flushes at the thought. Crap. Let's hope he's not a mind-reader.

Desperate to find something to say, to take my mind off him and Tilly, I run through in my mind the movies he's been in and remember the most recent one. "I remember you in *Lani Goes West*. You played Harry, the bad guy. Loved that movie."

"You got it." He flashes a perfect movie star smile. Not that I'd expect anything else.

Thank goodness I was right about him as Harry. Some of these movie stars are so touchy about their work, and if he starts moaning about me to Tilly...well, that would be all I need.

"It's my favorite out of all of Tilly's movies."

"You've seen them all?" He raises an eyebrow, like it's really weird for someone to admit to that. I know she's made over twenty movies, but that's not many for a true fan to see. Plus, it's been over a long period of time.

"Um...yes. We all have over the years, from when we were young."

"We?"

"My friends. We love Tilly, I mean her movies." If I don't watch it, he'll have me labeled as one of those crazy obsessed fans. "Is that okay?"

"Yes, of course. And I can see you mean it, not like some jerks in the business who'll stab you in the back quicker than look at you, given the opportunity."

Sounds like he's talking from personal experience. Poor him, it must be hard playing second fiddle to Tilly. His time will come, I'm sure. How could it not, looking like he does? From now on I'll definitely follow his career.

"Do you think we should be getting back to the set? Zac might suddenly decide he needs me. I should really be in the resting tent," I say, reluctant to leave but not wanting to get into trouble.

"I hope you're not just saying that to get away from me." He winks, and my insides go all warm and squidgy.

How could he even think that? I'd love to spend more time getting to know him, if I could. What started out as being a very so-so day, especially with Tilly's insult, is fast becoming the best day I've had on set so far. "No. Of course not. It's because...well, you know Zac. He can get so...so..."

"Abi, chill. Don't be so uptight, it will be fine."

Easy for him to say; he's not working here. Then again, maybe I am overreacting. It wouldn't be the first time. "Yes, I know. Sorry," I say.

"Come on, we'll go back together." He holds out his arm.

I think he wants me to link mine through his, and as I tentatively wrap my fingers around his bicep, my heart skips a beat, and a feeling of warmth shoots through me.

...

Standing in line at the craft service table waiting for lunch, my pulse quickens as I notice Jon a few people in front of me. I've been hoping to see him since we met the other day, only he hasn't been around. Not that I expect him to talk to me.

"Hey, watch what you're doing." The sound of an angry voice distracts me, and I stick my head out of the line to see what's going on.

Zac's first assistant, Chad, is glaring at one of the new interns. Judging by the OJ stain on his tee shirt and the upturned glass, she knocked his tray and sent his drink flying all over him.

"I'm sorry," she says, her bottom lip trembling.

I'd love to go over and give her a hug. I know how scary it can be here when you're new, and that's when everything's going well. To screw up takes newbie nerves off the scale. At least, it does in my world.

"Sorry isn't going to fix it. Get me another juice and then go find me another shirt."

She looks anxiously at the tray she's holding, which has a plate of salad on it, and then back at Chad. Indecision is written across her face.

"Leave the girl alone, Chad," Jon says, stepping out of line and striding toward them. "It was an accident, and you're upsetting her."

The intern goes crimson. "It's okay," she mutters, her

voice hardly audible. "It was my fault for not looking."

"Exactly," Chad says, narrowing his eyes.

Jon takes the intern's tray. "I'll get Chad's OJ. You go to wardrobe and find a clean tee. We'll leave your lunch at the end of the table by the cutlery." He flashes her a warm smile, and she mutters thanks and scuttles off. Jon then leans across some people in line and pulls out another OJ and places it on Chad's tray.

"Here. An orange juice. No harm done."

He's right. It's not like Chad was wearing something special. It's just a tee shirt with the movie name on it. We've all got one. There are probably boxes of them stashed away somewhere on the lot.

"I suppose not," Chad says, having the decency to look just a little embarrassed by his diva fit.

Jon steps back in line and acts like nothing just happened. I don't consider it nothing. I love that he stood up to Chad and didn't let him walk all over the intern.

It only takes a couple of minutes more until I have my lunch. Glancing around at the tables, I see Jon sitting alone, but can't bring myself to ask to join him, in case he says no. So instead I head toward Vince and the other guys but walk close to Jon's table, looking in front of me and acting like I don't know he's there.

"Abi," Jon calls as I'm walking past.

"Hi," I say trying to sound surprised to see him.

"Sit with me." He pats the chair beside him.

"Sure." I place my tray on the table and sit. My insides are tingling with the excitement of spending some more time with him. "It was so nice of you to stand up for the new intern like that," I say.

"It's hard when you're new somewhere," Jon says shrugging. "There's always someone trying to put you down."

"Tell me about it." I'm just about to say it's happened to me with Tilly, but luckily I check myself. It's one thing to agree with him on a general level, but to mention his girlfriend is quite another. To be honest, when I'm with Jon, I'd rather pretend Tilly doesn't even exist.

. . .

"Matt. Liv. Over here," I yell, running toward them as they get out of the car.

I promised them both a look around the set. Filming has finished for the day, so we won't be getting in the way. It'll be good to catch up. It seems like forever since we were all together. The movie seems to be taking up all my time. Not that I'm complaining. I love it.

"Hey," Liv says giving me a hug. "I can't believe we're going to see the actual set. Are they filming at the moment?" She looks around, her gaze darting from side to side as she checks everything out.

"No, it's over for the day, but I can show you where

it all happens." I walk between them both and link my arms through theirs.

"Are the actors still here? Tilly or Nathan?" Liv asks, sounding hopeful.

It feels weird, me being the one taking charge. Usually, when it's the three of us, Liv takes the lead. Not that I mind. I'm happy for her to do it.

"They might be. I'm not sure."

"If they are, can we meet them?" she pleads.

I'd be happy to introduce them to Nathan. Tilly? Well, let's hope we don't see her, because I don't want her making me look like a fool in front of Matt and Liv.

"Listen to you being all star-struck," Matt says. "They're only people, you know."

"Of course, you wouldn't want to meet Tilly Watson, if you had the chance," Liv retorts, glaring at him.

"Stop it, both of you. Or the tour ends, now." I try to sound annoyed, but they're making me laugh so much.

We head past the make-up and wardrobe trailers and down a short path into a big open space with buildings in the middle. "Here's the main set. Actually they are partial sets. On this side is Hui's village, and from the other side it's Wairere's village."

We walk around the set of Hui's village, which is just a collection of five houses that look like they're made from straw.

"Where do you ride the motorcycles?" Matt asks, scanning the area.

"Over on the other side of the field," I say, pointing in the distance. "Go and have a look. They might still be out if one of the technicians is working on them."

"Cool." He runs off, and I turn to Liv.

"Quick. Before Matt gets back, I want to tell you about Jon."

"Jon?" Liv frowns.

"He's Tilly's boyfriend. He's such a nice guy. And when he kissed me, I thought…"

"WHAT?" Liv hollers. "Back up a bit, missy. You've kissed Tilly's boyfriend, and you're only just telling me about it?"

Her eyes lock with mine, but I can't return the gaze and look down. My fists are balled. I should have called or text her. But I just wanted to keep it to myself for a while longer. Re-live what happened, even though it only lasted a few seconds. I can still put myself back into the scene and can even smell his cologne. It was light but enough to act like a drug on me. The way I'm starting to feel about him definitely seems different from the feelings I've had for Matt. And I'm glad, because I need to keep Matt firmly in the friend zone if I don't want him to panic and eventually run.

"Sorry. But I'm telling you now. I was in full make-up, and he thought I was Tilly. It was amazing. And when he found out his mistake, he didn't just ignore me. He acted as though he was glad it happened. I'd love for you to meet him."

"But he's Tilly's boyfriend." Liv frowns. "How could you do that to her?"

"I'm not doing anything." Even if part of me would like something to happen between us.

"Abi, just be careful." Liv chews on her bottom lip.

I know she means well, but there's nothing to be careful about.

"I will. Promise. Let's talk about something more exciting," I say wanting to change the subject. "Like your party. Any news?"

Liv's eyes light up. "Yes. Mom's agreed to ask my aunt if we can use their house. I'm sure she'll say yes. We can have the music in the barn and a barbecue by the pool. We'll have to hire a DJ."

"Aren't you leaving it a bit late for that? Over the summer they probably get booked up way in advance."

"Yeah, I know. Hey. I've just had an idea."

"Tell me."

"You can say no. I will understand, I promise. But…"

"Come on. Spit it out, girl."

"You could invite all the guys from the movie. Vince and the others. Do you think they'd come?"

To a party for an eighteen year old? I don't think so. "I'm not sure," I say instead. "They don't go out much because filming starts so early in the morning. But I can ask."

"And, there's Tilly," adds Liv. "I know you said she can be really nasty sometimes, but if she would come, that would make my party the most sought after place to be, and I wouldn't invite any of the popular people. That would be so funny. Let them know what it's like to be on the outside for a change."

Tilly at Liv's party. That's so insane it's not even worth thinking about. Not that she'd ever consider going. I'd stake my life on it.

"Leave it to me. Let's go and find Matt."

We bump into him on our way to the field.

"There wasn't anyone there," Matt says, looking despondent.

"Sorry. They've probably put everything away for the night. Do you want to check out wardrobe and make-up? And then we can go to craft services and see if there's anyone around."

"Okay," Liv says.

She definitely doesn't seem as excited as when we met. I guess the tour is a bit of a letdown. When filming isn't going on, there's not a lot happening.

We walk in silence toward the trailers when in the distance I see Jon standing on his own.

"There's Jon. Do you want to meet him?" I ask Liv and then instantly regret it, in case she accidentally says something to him she shouldn't. Then I get annoyed with myself for thinking that. She's hardly going to tell Jon how I feel. Just as long as she doesn't tell Matt, though.

"Sure."

We walk over to him, and the closer we get, the faster

my heart races, until we're actually in front of him, and I can hardly process my thoughts.

"Hi, Jon. These are my friends, Liv and Matt."

Jon shakes hands with Matt and takes Liv's hand and kisses it. How cute is that?

"So has the lovely Abi been showing you around the set?"

A shiver runs down my spine listening to him calling me lovely.

"Yes. It's awesome," Liv replies.

"Here's Tilly," I say seeing Tilly making her way to where we're standing.

I feel Liv's body tense next to me. It's exciting for her to finally meet Tilly, whatever I've been saying about her.

"Hi Tilly," I say as she gets close to us.

"Let's get out of here," she says to Jon, totally ignoring me.

"Abi just said hello," he responds.

"Hello," Tilly says, casting a quick glance in my direction before turning back to Jon. "I could murder a vodka-martini. Several in fact. After the day I've had, I intend to get wasted." She turns and leaves, with Jon following.

My eyes are fixed on their retreating backs. Well, on Jon's really. I love how he wasn't going to let her ignore me. I like him more and more every time I see him.

"Damn. I was just about to ask them about my

party," Liv says, acting like we didn't just get blown off by Tilly.

"I don't think it was the right time. Sorry about the way she acted," I say, dragging my thoughts from Jon.

"Well, it's not easy being in the limelight all the time. I feel sorry for her," Liv says.

"Hmm. You wouldn't if you had her getting on your case most of the time," I say.

"So quit," Matt says.

Liv and I both stare at him. What is this boy on? Why would he suggest that?

"Why would she do that?" Liv asks, echoing my thoughts.

"Yes, *why*?" I add.

"If it's as bad as you say, what's the point in doing it anymore? And they're so fake. Especially that Jon." He shrugs.

"I didn't say it was bad, just that sometimes Tilly can be difficult to work with. Anyway, I'm not with her all the time. And Jon's definitely not fake." He wouldn't think that about Jon if he got to know him better. And more importantly, if I left, I wouldn't see Jon any more. That more than makes up for how Tilly treats me.

"If you say so," says Matt. "And what about how she pokes fun at the way you speak? Is that okay?" His eyes lock with mine. I shouldn't have told him she did that, because he'll never let it go. "Because I don't think it is," he adds, his voice softer and a look of concern on his face. He's so sweet, always looks out for me. But in this case, he doesn't need to be so worried.

I bow my head. "Of course it's not, and she doesn't do it all the time. Anyway, no way will I quit. It's the best job ever."

Chapter Ten

"Anyone seen Tilly?" Zac yells.

She's picked a fine time to go AWOL. Zac's in one hell of a mood this morning, because yesterday's rushes were a disaster. I'm not sure why. All I know is it's enough to set us back even more. As long as I finish filming before college starts, that's the main thing. I don't like my chances if I have to tell Mom I'm going to be missing classes.

"Abi, go and see if Tilly's in make-up or wardrobe," Zac says. "If she is, tell her to get her butt down here pronto so we can re-shoot the love scene. If she isn't, phone the hotel and see if she's there."

That's great. Why me? He has his own assistant. Not that she's around either, for some reason. Maybe it's a conspiracy.

"Okay," I reply, but Zac doesn't seem to be listening as he's already walking towards the other side of the set.

"While we're waiting, Nathan," I hear Zac say. "Let's do a quick run through of the scene where you're preparing for the fight on the Tamaki plain."

I half walk and half run in the direction of make-up. Please let her be there. I don't want to phone the hotel. I hate calling strange places in case I get my words all mixed up.

"Abi." Jon strides toward me, and I get a fluttery feeling in my stomach. My heart goes into double-flip mode. I wonder if this will always happen every time I see him.

"Hey," I say, trying to sound casual. "I didn't know you were back." He's only been gone for a few days, but it's seemed like forever.

"Just I thought I'd surprise Tilly as she's not expecting me until tomorrow. I popped into the hotel, but she's not there." Yay! At least that saves me a phone call.

"Zac sent me to look for her. I guess she must be in make-up or wardrobe if she's not there. He wants her on set right away. We've got to re-shoot some of yesterday's scenes."

"I'll walk with you." He turns and we start to walk, fairly slowly, which is worrying seeing as Zac's waiting. Then again, the chance to be alone with Jon isn't something that happens often. And Zac won't know what I'm doing. "So, tell me how it's going? Is Tilly behaving her-self?" I stop in my tracks and look at him. His eyes fix on mine, and my knees wobble. "It's okay," he says. "I know she can be a handful. We've worked together be-fore. But she doesn't mean it; she's quite insecure under-neath it all. I guess you already know that."

Um…no. That part of her nature must have passed me by. Even if he isn't the first person to mention it.

"Sure. Things are good. We're behind on the sched-ule, but nobody, apart from Zac, seems upset."

"Movies always run over. Don't worry—it means you get paid more, so that's got to be a plus."

"Definitely. I'm saving up to go to Europe next summer." He doesn't need to know that our trip is more a dream than a reality.

"Europe," he says, giving a low whistle.

"Yes, with my friend Liv." I shrug, like it's no big deal.

"You should come to L.A. I could show you around."

Is he serious? That would be like…like…

"Thanks. But I'll have to talk to Liv about it. We've sort of already planned on Europe."

I'm sure Liv would think L.A. is as exciting as London. She'd love it, checking out all the celebrity houses. Wandering down Rodeo Drive. It would be awesome.

"When you decide, let me know. How about you check make-up, and I check wardrobe? One of us will find her, doing whatever she shouldn't be, knowing Tilly. We'll meet back here."

My heart plummets once I realize we're here. I'd really love to keep on talking to him.

"Okay."

I push open the door and look around. It's empty. Suddenly, I hear a strange muffled sound coming from the back of the room. "Hello," I call. "Tilly, is that you?" I don't know what made me think it's her. A gut feeling, I guess.

There's no answer, but when I get to the closet door, I can definitely hear something going on. I knock gently, but nobody answers. So I slowly turn the handle. God knows what I'm going to find. I'd like to run in the opposite direction, but I don't want to feel the full force of Zac's temper, which I will if Tilly's in here and I don't speak to her.

I push open the door very gently and see Tilly's profile as she's locking lips with...

Dean. Tilly's PR guy's assistant.

It's ridiculous that I'm standing here watching Dean and Tilly all over each other, while Jon is outside looking for her. How could Tilly do this to Jon? Anyone could have found them. Even Jon. And by the looks of things, they clearly haven't even realized I'm standing here.

Talk about stepping into a situation I *do not* want to be in.

What am I supposed to do now?

I cough. "Tilly." She doesn't reply, just waves a dismissive hand in my direction and carries on kissing Dean.

My fists are balled by my side. I could swing at her. I really could.

"Tilly," I repeat, trying to sound firm.

She pulls away from Dean and glares at me. "What?"

"Zac wants you on set to film the love scene again. The rushes from yesterday are no good. He wants you there *now*." I narrow my eyes to try and accentuate how important it is.

"Whatever," she growls. "I'll be there in a minute."

Without replying, I turn and walk away, back to where I left Jon, and notice him coming in the opposite direction.

"Did you find her?" Jon asks.

What the hell am I supposed to say? That Tilly's only a few yards away, hooking up with some guy? If I do tell him, what's he gonna do? Punch Dean? Storm off and leave the set? Break down and need me to comfort him? Okay, so the last one is in my dreams.

If I don't tell him, will Tilly say that I saw her? Then he'll know I lied to him. But I can say I didn't want him to get hurt.

I clench my teeth in frustration. Talk about being stuck between a rock and a hard place. "No. I-I-I take it you d-d-didn't either?"

Jon averts his eyes, a typical reaction. Damn my stutter. I hope he doesn't suspect me of lying. Especially as I usually don't stutter in front of him now.

"So where is she?" Jon frowns.

All I want to do is shout in his ear, *In wardrobe cheating on you, that's where*. But of course I don't.

"Maybe she went for a walk by the river," I suggest, anxious to get him away from here in case Tilly emerges with Dean. Although that would solve the problem. It would also upset Jon, and the fallout could totally ruin today's shoot.

"Okay, let's go there," Jon says.

"If you think Zac won't mind," I say, suddenly remembering him, as I've been off set for quite a while now. Though hopefully he *won't* mind since he was the one who asked me to find her. If it takes longer than it should, it's not my fault.

"If he does, he'll get over it. Come on, live a little. Tilly will appear in her own good time. She usually does." His lips turn up in a lazy smile, and my insides go all squidgy. My knees feel like they're about to give way. "Anyway, while we're on our way, I want to ask you a favor."

He holds out his hand. But before taking it, I quickly scan where we are to make sure no one can see. Realizing it's all clear, I put my hand in his. His palm is smooth and soft. Warm but not sweaty. Perfect like the rest of him. My heart is thumping so loudly against my ribcage that it will be a miracle if Jon doesn't hear it.

"Sure. What is it?" I ask, imagining all sorts of things that I've dreamed of him asking, but knowing it's gonna be something like collect his cleaning or something equally boring.

"I've got an audition coming up and wondered if you could teach me some fighting skills? You make it look so easy."

I wasn't expecting that. Teaching him how to fight. A gift. Something I could do in my sleep, and do it well. Then he'll see me confident and in control. And completely stutter-free. I can't wait.

"Yeah, of course. Just let me know where and when," I say trying to sound cool about it, but inside my stomach is doing somersaults, I'm so excited at the thought of it.

Spending time alone with Jon. What more could I ask for? I guess some people, probably Matt, would say I'm behaving no better than Tilly, but that's not true. It's not like we're hooking up. I'm doing him a favor, because I have the skills, and he doesn't.

• • •

"Come on Abi, spill," says Vince when we're sitting outside together on one of the wooden benches overlooking the hills, eating our lunch.

"Spill what?" I ask, frowning. Surely he doesn't

mean about me teaching Jon, because how on earth would he know about it? Then again, if he knew about it, he wouldn't be asking me to spill. So I still don't get it.

"Don't act all Miss Innocent with me. Ever since you came back from your Tilly hunt earlier, it's been like working with a zombie. You've barely said two words to me. To any of us."

Oh. And I thought I'd managed to act normally. It's just that I can't stop thinking about everything. And I can't tell Vince about me and Jon. Not that I've agreed to teach him or that we held hands and walked to the river. Or that I pretended not to find Tilly.

"I don't want to say." I inwardly slap myself on the head. Why didn't I just say there was nothing wrong? Because now he knows something's up.

"What'd she say?"

"Who?"

"Tilly. This has to be about something she said to you. How any times do I have to tell you to ignore it? She's always the same; she'll pick on the person she believes is the weakest. It's what bullies do."

How does he know all this stuff? You know I'd love it if I could get him and Liv together. They'd get along so well. Maybe I can do something about it at the party.

"If I tell you, you have to promise not to say anything to anyone." Could I sound any more like a third-grader? "When I was looking for Tilly, I found her in wardrobe with Dean." That's all I'm saying. I won't mention spending time with Jon at all.

"Yeah, we know all about them."

"Well, I didn't," I snap.

"Whoa," Vince says, holding both hands up. "It's no big deal. Tilly's always hooking up with someone. Anyway, why did it affect you like that?"

"Because Jon was around, and I didn't want him to see."

Vince rests his arm on mine. "You're too nice, that's your trouble. What happens between Jon and Tilly is their business. You can't worry about him seeing her with Dean. That's for her to deal with and not for you to get upset over."

"Yeah, I guess." But all the same, I don't believe him. Jon deserves much better than that.

Chapter Eleven

"There you are," Matt says, walking toward me. "I've been waiting forever. I thought you said to pick you up at five."

I swallow hard. Crap. Make that double crap. I totally forgot to text him.

"I'm so sorry. I agreed to give Jon some basic fighting training for his next movie audition. I've been meaning to text you all day, but it's just been so crazy here. I'm really sorry."

"I can wait." He shrugs. "I'll come and watch."

Noooooooo. I don't want Jon and Matt to be together. It's just not right.

"It's fine. Jon doesn't want anyone to know I'm teaching him. I'll get a ride home with someone else. Or call a cab. I'm really sorry."

A sad expression crosses Matt's face, and a pang of guilt shoots through me. I feel like I'm bailing on him, but I agreed to help Jon. And I want to. Matt will get over it. Our friendship's too strong for him to hold it against me.

"Okay. See ya." Matt turns and leaves.

I watch for a moment, and then walk to the bathroom to check myself out before I go to meet Jon.

He's waiting for me by the river just like we arranged. He thought it was sufficiently out of the way to make sure the others don't see us. I'm not sure why he wants to keep it secret, unless he's worried I'll be breaking my contract, but it's not like we're going to fight. I'm just going to give him some tips.

"Hey, look at you," Jon says walking toward me. "Had a good day?" He rests his arm across my shoulders and gives a gentle squeeze. My nerve endings tingle, and butterflies whizz around my stomach. I try to remind myself that actors like to touch everyone, but somehow this seems different.

"Yeah."

"Come on then, show me what to do. I don't have to fight hard, just look like I know what I'm doing."

He drops his arm, and I take a step forward and turn to face him.

"Okay. First of all you need to stand like this." I move my legs until they're about three feet apart and then bend my knees doing several gentle bounces.

Jon copies. "Like this?" he asks.

"Perfect. If you maintain this stance all the time, it will make it easy for you to move quickly. See?" I dart in front, to the side and then to the back all the time coming back to the same place and keeping my knees bent and my body relaxed. "You try."

Jon tries it, but he's not a natural. Each move seems forced. He doesn't have the fluidity that Matt does, and I make him practice it for several more minutes before deciding that it's time to move on.

"Okay. That's good. The next thing you have to do is always keep your guard." I bring my hands up and tuck in my elbows. "You try." Jon bring up his hands, but his elbows stick out, so I go over to him and take hold of his arms and position them correctly. I allow myself a moment to enjoy his closeness, and the hairs on the back of my neck stand up. "Now you can block any punches." I step away from him. "Drop your elbows to deflect a body shot. And this," I lift up my elbows and reach my hand over to touch my ear, "to block a head shot."

"I can see why you were chosen to double for Tilly. You make it look so easy," Jon says, admiration showing in his eyes.

This is turning out to be the most perfect day ever. "I-I train hard," I say, angry with myself for stuttering. "The last thing I want to show you is how to dodge."

"I want to fight, not dodge," Jon says frowning.

"Dodging is part of it. If you block, you can hurt

your arm. If you dodge, you don't get hurt."

"Oh. I get it," he says. Basic stuff, but he seems really impressed.

"Plus, it's much easier to attack your opponent right after their attack if you've dodged than if you block. I'll show you. Take a swing at me."

He looks shocked. "You want me to punch you?"

I try to suppress a laugh. I can just imagine Matt's face if he was listening. Jon's got no chance against me. He's not fast by any stretch of the imagination.

"I want you to try." I don't tell him that I could beat him with my eyes closed, because that's not exactly going to win him over. And I love that he's showing admiration for my skills.

"Ooo-kay." He shakes his head, then lifts his arm and aims a punch at me.

I step to the left, avoiding his weak shot and then go to hit him, my fist stopping just short of connecting with his chest. "See what I mean?" I ask, smirking at him.

"Oh yes," Jon says stepping toward me and taking hold of my hand. "I see."

My heart does a triple-flip, and all I can do is stare at him. I think he's gonna kiss me. He is. He definitely is.

Then his cell rings, and he takes it out his pocket and looks at the caller ID. "Sorry, I have to take this. It might take a while. I'll see you later."

He turns his back and walks away, leaving me alone.

The moment is gone.

. . .

"You won't believe the way Mom and Dad were act-ing earlier," I tell Liv and Matt as we're walking toward Starbucks after class. I agreed to help out with the ju-niors again. Earlier I was going to call Bill and say I couldn't make it, but Mom and Dad went nuts at me for even thinking about it.

I texted Liv and asked her to meet us, since I didn't feel like going home as soon as class was over, not after what happened. And I brought Mom's car, so it's not like I have to be back at any time. Well, as long as I'm not out after eleven.

"What did they do?" says Liv looking concerned.

"What they said, more like. Moaning about me not wanting to come to class to help Bill and my attitude and stuff. Just because I said I was tired and wanted to skip tonight. And then they started going on about how much I was letting Bill down, and you too, Matt. I mean, it's not like I do it a lot, is it?" I notice out the corner of my eye Matt is nodding. "I don't. So stop nodding like that." I scowl at Matt. And he scowls in return.

Great. That's all I need. What is it with everyone?

"Let's put it this way," Matt says. "Since this movie thing started, you haven't been the same."

What is his deal? Of course I've been the same. Okay, so I'm not around as much as I used to be, but that doesn't mean I've changed. All it means is that I'm busy. So sue me.

"That is such freakin' crap. Have you got a hotline to my parents, or something? Anyway, I've hardly seen you because of all the hours we've been working. So how can you say that? I'm the same as I've always been. You tell me how I'm different. Go on."

I glare at him, and he then averts his eyes and looks at Liv, who shrugs. He scowls.

"I go to pick you up from the set, and you blow me off."

"Once. That happened. Once. And I said sorry." He's deliberately focusing on one thing and not remembering everything else where I am exactly as I've always been.

"You didn't turn up to meet us twice recently without even texting." Okay. There were those two times as well. But that's it.

"I'm sorry, but I couldn't help that. It's not my fault if Zac decides to have extra rehearsals right at the last minute, is it? I don't have my cell on set with me, so I couldn't tell you."

"Maybe not, but even when we do see you, your mind's elsewhere. You said you would help Bill with the juniors, but when you're there, it's like you're just going through the motions and would rather be somewhere else. Everyone's noticed."

This is getting worse by the minute. Now I'm the subject of a gripefest by the dojo members. That's just great. Well, if you ask me, they're just jealous because they're not in a movie like I am.

"Well, I couldn't care less about everyone else. None of you understand what it's like working all these hours then having to go to the dojo. And then have your parents get on you like you're some sort of dropout with no c-c-conscience."

"I think we do understand," says Matt. "You don't stop talking about it. Vince this, Vince, that. Zac this, Zac that. And as for Tilly and now this"—he gestures wildly in front of him as if he can barely bring himself to say the name—"Jon."

Is Matt on a roll, or what? I can't remember hearing him so passionate about anything since…well, ever.

"Matt, enough," says Liv. She holds up her hand to silence him. "Can't you see Abi's upset?" Just as she says this we reach Starbucks, so we go in and, while Liv and I grab a table, Matt goes to order.

"Thanks," I say. "What's gotten into him, going off on me like that?"

"Abi, don't take this the wrong way." She pauses a moment and chews on her bottom lip. "But, Matt's sort of right. You're not the same as you used to be. I know it's all exciting working on a movie, the sort of thing everyone dreams about…"

"Except me," I say interrupting.

Liv snorts. "Except you. Yes. And you're one who ends up with the chance. Freakin' typical, if you ask me."

The irony of the situation certainly isn't lost on me.

"But if I'd known what it was like, then I'd probably have dreamed about it too. I'm sorry if I keep going on about it. It's hard not to. I'll try to stop though, promise. I didn't realize I'd gotten so bad."

"It's okay. And don't mind Matt. I think he's jealous."

"Well, he could have hardly done stunt work for Tilly, could he?"

"Not of that," Liv says giggling.

"What, then?"

"Your new friends. We both are, I guess. Suddenly you don't need us like before." She drops her head, her mouth twisted in a sad little frown.

How can they think that? We've been friends for years, and I've never minded when Liv's had other friends. Well, not too much. Apart from the time she started to spend a lot of time with this girl Tess. Then I really felt left out.

"I'm sorry," I say guilt flooding through me. "I didn't mean for you to feel like that.," I rest my hand on her arm. "You're my best friends. You know you are."

"Yes, of course we do. We'll get used to it. This new, confident you."

"I wouldn't go that far. More confident than I used to be, but I'm not you. Never will be.

"Fraps all round," says Matt, putting our drinks on the table.

"Thanks." I give him a huge smile. "And sorry for being such a jerk," I add, even if I don't agree that I have been. But it's worth saying sorry to keep being friends. The thought of falling out with him for good hurts more than I even want to admit.

"Don't sweat it," he says. And he winks at me. I guess things are back to normal if Matt's flirting again. I knew apologizing would do the trick.

Chapter Twelve

I came in early today to see Doug, from craft services, about a DJ for Liv's party. She's had no luck finding anyone, and I remember him saying his partner was one. Liv's other problem is that she also doesn't have much money to spend.

"Leave it to me," Doug says after I ask him. "We'll find someone for you."

"Thanks, so much. I really appreciate it."

Walking away, I pull out my phone to text Liv. She'll never believe it. Actually, I think I'll call her. This is too important for a text. I hope she's not asleep, not that she'll mind me waking her when it's something this big.

I punch in her number, and after three rings she answers.

"Abi?" Her voice sounds all sleepy and hoarse.

"Yeah. Sorry to wake you, but you won't mind when I tell you why."

"Don't bet on it. I didn't get to bed until two last night," she groans.

"Two? How come?"

"Matt and I went to the movies, and we bumped into a couple of his friends from school. Rich and Sam, do you know them? We all ended up at Matt's, where I crashed. Where I still am."

My body clenches. I don't believe it. Liv went to the movies with Matt and then stayed at his house. And they didn't invite me. Since when have they started to go out together without me? What's going on? It's always the three of us. Or me and Liv at school. Or me and Matt at the dojo. It's never just Liv and Matt. Never. I'm the person that links us. It's always been like that.

And how come Liv's parents are okay with her sleeping at his house? How well do they know him? Has he spent lots of time at her house with her parents? Why am I feeling like crap about this?

"B-but why d-d-didn't you ask me? I wasn't doing anything last night." I try not to sound like a petulant child, but I don't think I'm succeeding.

"Abi, I'm so sorry. We didn't mean anything by it. We just thought you'd be filming. You've been a bit incommunicado recently." She lets out a long yawn. "Come on, what have you got to tell me?"

Suddenly the news doesn't seem that exciting, not when you compare it to getting blown off by your supposed best friends.

"Just about a DJ for the party, it's all sorted." I say in a monotone voice.

"Abi, you rock!" Suddenly Liv sounds wide awake and very excited.

"Yeah."

Does she expect me to be all *yay how awesome* now? Because it's not gonna happen.

"Hey. What's wrong? One minute you're all excited about it, and now you're acting like it's nothing. It's last night, isn't it?" she asks before I have time to reply.

"No." I can practically feel my bottom lip jutting out in one massive pout.

"Come on, Abi, this is me you're talking to. You're in a bad mood because we didn't invite you to the movies." She knows me so well.

"I'm not." I pause for a moment. "Okay, I am. We always go together."

"Look, I'm really sorry, but it wasn't planned. I was in town doing some shopping and saw Matt, who was doing the same. Anyway, we decided on the spur of the moment to go. No biggie."

Well, if that's what happened, maybe I am overreacting a bit. But even so, they could've have thought of me. How long does it take to text someone? Then again, it depends on how long they had until the movie started, and I probably wouldn't have made it in time. "Sorry. Don't mind me. I'm just being stupid."

What if Liv and Matt get together? Like as in *really* get together. I don't think I could stand it. Because it's obvious what would happen to our friendship. It would be over. However much they said otherwise, I'd really be on the outside.

Unless something happened with me and Jon, and then it wouldn't matter so much. We could be a foursome.

"Rich is so hot. Isn't he?" She giggles. "I'm going to ask him to the party. Do you think he'll come?"

Rich? So she's not thinking about Matt in that way at all. That's a relief. I wonder if she'd tell me if she was, though.

If Jon was my boyfriend, he'd understand about my friendship with Matt. He'd understand about my other friendships, too. I give a loud sigh. Thinking about Jon always makes me do that. Every day, I hope that he'll end it with Tilly, because of the way she treats him, and then he'll want to be with me.

"What does that loud sigh mean?" Liv asks. "You don't think Rich will want to come."

Ooops, I really should concentrate more.

"Sorry. No. I was thinking about something else. Yes, I'm sure he will. Mention it to Matt."

"Okay. And if I say that Tilly's coming to the party, he's bound to say yes."

I wish she'd give up on this idea, because it just isn't gonna happen. Not that Tilly even knows about the party.

"No. We don't know that she'll be coming."

"Have you asked her yet?"

It's not like we sit and talk all the time. "N-not yet. The time hasn't been right. You know how she is. I can't just go up to her and ask. I did mention the party to some of the others, but they're not sure. It all depends on how behind schedule we are. There have been a few problems."

"Don't worry. I know you'll get them there if you can."

"Sure. And even if Tilly can't make it, hopefully Jon might. I'll ask him later. If he says yes then you'll be able to meet him for longer than a few seconds. I've been teaching him some fighting moves." I can't help the corners of my mouth turning up into a slight smile.

We've hardly had chance to talk about Jon, because our calls have been short or Matt's been with us. I don't want him to know. I'm not sure why. Actually, I am. It's because Matt will say something about Jon being Tilly's boyfriend, and that I should stay clear of him. It's easy for him to say that, because he doesn't understand the whole situation. And if I try to tell him, he'll just mock me.

"Teaching him fighting skills, huh? Just be careful. Remember he's still with Tilly. You know, I can't believe that you'd even think about stealing someone's boyfriend. That is so not you." If I could see her, I just know she'd be shaking her head.

"I'm not. I just like him. That's all. A lot. She can be so awful to him. He's a cool guy. You'll see."

"I repeat. Just be careful. I don't like your chances if Tilly finds out you're after him. Anyway, he might say yes to the party and bring her."

That thought had crossed my mind, but I ignored it. As I did with the thought that I can't just invite him without her.

"I will. Don't worry," I say, not sure whether I'm trying to convince her or myself.

"After you first told me about him, I googled him and then I remembered," Liv says. "He played Harry in *Lani Goes West*. Hot to look at, but a crap actor. Do you remember? We kept mocking his accent, a mixture of *The Sopranos* meets *Deadwood*." Liv giggles.

Oh yes, I'd forgotten. Now I feel really mean. We did make fun of him, but I'm sure he wasn't as bad as Liv remembers, and it's hard for someone from the UK to do an American accent—at least, that's what Jon told me. I'll take another look at the movie when I get home.

"I expect he was told to speak like that by the director," I say with an edge to my voice. "And if the director was like Zac, Jon wouldn't have had a say in it."

"Sorry, I didn't mean to upset you. I was just being dumb. Is he in your movie too?" Liv asks.

"No, he's between jobs at the moment. Although he's going back to L.A. soon for the audition."

"As long as it's not for a cowboy, he should be okay." She giggles, then it goes muffled like she's put her hand over her mouth to stop herself in case it upsets me. Which it doesn't.

"I know what you're doing. And I'm not upset by you laughing. I was just being supersensitive before. Ignore me."

"Okay, if you insist. Look, I better go. I've got to go home in a minute because Mom's book club is meeting at our house this afternoon, and she wants a hand with preparing the food. But, before I do, what are you wearing to the party and what time will you be at my place? We'll have to allow a couple of hours to set everything up."

Why did she have to bring that up now? She's going to kill me when I tell her.

"I might have to meet you at your aunt's house. We're filming, and I'm not sure what time I can get away because we're so far behind. Zac's said we have to be prepared to work late."

"You're kidding?" Her voice drops, and I feel terrible, letting her down like this.

"I'll try my hardest to get to your house first. But if not, I'll see you at your aunt's. I'll text you and let you know how it's going. Sorry, but I'll get there as soon as I can and hopefully bring some guests, promise."

• • •

"Remember the set-up," Zac calls.

He's standing behind the camera, ready to shoot the scene where Wairere rescues Hui from his burning motorcycle. We've rehearsed it lots of times, and I've worked with Danny to make sure it's right. The one thing he told me was to stay calm and remember to breathe.

"Ready," I shout.

"Action."

Adrenaline courses through my veins as I run in the direction of Hui, who's trapped under the bike. When I get to within a couple feet of him, I leap in the air and kick out with my leg, pushing the bike away so it's on the ground next to him. The heat from the flames is intense, even though I'm covered in a protective gel, and my clothes are flame resistant, and it's hard to breathe. I push these thoughts to the back of my mind and grab hold of Hui's arms and drag him away to safety.

"Cut," Zac hollers. "Good job."

I become aware of the sound of everyone applauding. I glance up and see them all looking in my direction. I can't help smiling.

"Awesome," Vince says. "I couldn't have done it better myself."

I feel myself blush but don't care. To get that sort of praise from him is ridiculous, seeing as he's been a stunt double for years.

"Thanks," I reply, feeling about ten feet tall.

"You should think about making a career of it. You're a natural."

Only a few weeks ago I had no idea what to do with my life, and now it's like everything is falling into place. Doing the movie has given me a goal for my future. It's something I'm doing on my own without Mom and Dad or Liv and Matt interfering. Even if they do it with the best of intentions, it's good to know that I might be able to make it on my own.

"Thanks. That would be so cool."

Chapter Thirteen

"No. I won't."

Tilly sounds really angry; I wonder who she's going after this time. I didn't realize she knew about my hideaway in the woods. I often come here to get away from everything or to do some stretching between shooting. Maybe Jon mentioned it because I told him.

So, should I stay here behind the tree and listen, or go back? The trouble is that they might hear me if I move and think I'm spying on them. Which I am now, even if it is unintentional.

"You will do as I say, my girl, or you know the consequences."

What the…? No one in their right mind talks to Tilly like that.

"*Whatever.* Look Mom, you don't rule my life. Not anymore."

"Ohhhhhh," I say out loud, then quickly slam my hand over my mouth to stop them from hearing me. It's her mom. I've read in the magazines that she's the driving force behind Tilly's career and has been since Tilly was five.

"Do you want the media to find out about your latest exploits, like I made sure they did the last time?" her mom snaps. "If you don't, then you won't question my decisions. They are for your own good."

Nooooo. She's one of *those* moms. The kind who sell their kids out to the media. It's just wrong. Moms should protect you, not spill everything to the newspapers. How can she live with herself after doing something like that to her daughter? There's no way my mom would do anything like that to me. Ever.

"For the good of your pocket, you mean," Tilly growls.

"Watch your mouth. You will sign the contracts, and that's the end of it."

Man, I'm glad she's not my mother. How come Tilly lets her call the shots? She's over eighteen, plus with her money and lifestyle she can do whatever she wants. It doesn't make sense. Maybe her mom has got something on her. Something that could wreck her career. But it can't be that. No mom, even Tilly's, would use something against their own daughter. Maybe, deep down, it's because Tilly wants to please her mom like I want to please mine—most of the time. Although, in Tilly's case, it doesn't sound like it'll ever happen.

"Mom, three movies in a year is crazy. Not to mention all the publicity they get me to do. I need some time off."

"You'll have plenty of time off when the next bright young thing arrives on the scene. In the meantime, you work and work *hard.* If you need anything from my physician contacts to help keep you on top, you know I can arrange it."

Physician contacts? Does she mean drugs? I don't care how famous Tilly is. It's not right. Anyway, I can't stay and listen to this. I'm heading back. I turn and put one foot in front of the other as lightly as possible so they can't hear me.

After a few minutes, I see Vince heading in my direction. Another person who knows my secret place, which clearly isn't secret at all. I just thought it was because I've never seen anyone there before.

"Hey, Vince, don't go that way," I say, pointing toward the woods.

"Why not?"

"Tilly's there, having a shouting match with her mom."

"Ah, I was wondering when the infamous Renee would turn up." He grimaces.

"You know her then?"

"Everyone knows her. She makes periodic visits to

the set, when globe-trotting allows, creates as much stink as possible, then disappears." He shrugs. "I guess we'll all suffer once Renee goes, because Tilly's not going to be happy."

I feel sorry for Tilly. It can't be easy for her to have a mom like that. No wonder she acts like she does sometimes. It's not like she has a good role model.

Yikes, I'm sounding like Mom. Then again, that proves my point.

"Well, it must be hard for her. Moms aren't supposed to be like that."

"Oh, Abi. You're so sweet." He ruffles my hair, and I pull away. Unnecessarily messed-up hair doesn't go down too well with Mel. "Not everyone has a regular mom like yours."

"How do you know what my mom's like?"

"Because I hear you on the phone with her, and I've seen you together when she's picked you up from the set instead of Matt. We all have. Don't knock it. I bet Tilly would kill to have a mom like yours."

She would? Really? But if she had my mom, she wouldn't have been in the movies. She'd have had a normal life instead, and Tilly doesn't do normal. Why would she want to when she is worshipped wherever she goes?

Then again, maybe Vince has got a point. I don't know how I'd have coped without Mom being with me when things got tough. I'm not saying she isn't annoying sometimes, because there are times when she tries to tell me what to do and she seems to forget that I'm actually an adult. But I can talk to her about stuff and know that she'll support me. Not like Tilly's mom. According to the tabloids—and based off what I heard this afternoon— her agenda is all about the dollar, and if it means screwing over her daughter, well, then so what.

"Maybe." I see Tilly walking near a row of motorcycles, looking strangely withdrawn, the usual Tilly sparkle uncharacteristically subdued. I gesture in her direction. "I'm going to see if she's okay." I leave Vince and run over to her.

"Hi," I say.

"What do you want?" Tilly narrows her eyes and glares at me.

"I. I. h-h-heard you with your mom. And-and wondered if you were okay." Now that the words are out, they make me sound really lame.

She flinches, just a little, when I mention her mom. "Of course I'm okay. What's it to you?"

"N-n-nothing. I thought you might want to talk about it."

"Well, you thought wrong." Tilly storms off.

As I watch her retreat, it hits me, the reason why she's mean all the time. It's a defense mechanism. She's in pain and doesn't want anyone to find out. So she keeps people at a distance, being nasty to them so they don't even try to get close to her. It doesn't stop what she says to me from hurting, though. And it's still not right.

. . .

By the time Zac's finally happy with today's shoot, I realize it's way too late for me to go to Liv's house before the party. I texted a while ago to tell her we were way behind, and the response was terse, to say the least.

But it's not like I didn't warn her.

Anyway, I need to get home ASAP to shower and change. If I hurry I'll just make the nine-fifteen bus. I'd ask Matt to pick me up, but can't because I asked him to go early to the party since I couldn't. And I can't call Mom because she's busy tonight. Maybe I should get a cab, except it will cost about fifty dollars. I'm going to borrow Mom's car once I make it home to get to Liv's aunt's place. Liv said we can sleep over in their guestroom.

"Hey, Abi. You coming?" Jon's voice startles me. I didn't know he was on set, so unlike me not to notice him.

"Where?"

"The Tavern. Everyone's going. I figure they need it after today. Zac certainly got his money's worth out of you all."

"Sorry, going to a party," I say, wanting to scream in frustration. How unlucky can a girl be? Typical that they're going out tonight of all nights. The Tavern is an amazing place, not that I've ever been there before. Way out of my league, but if I were with everyone from here, it would be okay.

"Go later. Parties never warm up 'til the early hours." He gives one his knee-wobbling smiles, and my stomach goes all fluttery. I can't believe he really wants me to go with them. It's so tempting, and he's right about parties taking a while to get going.

I could just go for a little while and then head for the party. Hopefully, Liv will understand. It would just be so nice to spend some time with Jon. Anyway, he might want for me to go with them now, but once Tilly's around, he'll be with her and he won't be able to talk to me. So I probably won't even be that late.

"I'd love to, but I'm not sure. Even if I could go, I don't have anything to wear, I can hardly go like this." I glance down at my dress, which I love, but it's so not club gear.

"Borrow something else from wardrobe. Ask Fran."

He's making this so hard for me.

"It takes forever to get my make-up off. You'll be long gone by the time I'm ready."

"I'll wait for you." He grins, and my heart skips a beat.

"Won't Tilly mind?" I ask.

"Didn't I say? I thought I did. Tilly's not going. She's not feeling well. She's going back to the hotel, so you could stand in for her and be my partner. I promise to get you to the party later. I'll come with you, if you'd like."

If I like? Of course I freakin' well like. This is beyond anything I've ever imagined. How can I say no? Liv's got to understand, I'll text her and say I'm definitely coming, just a bit later than I thought. Actually, no I won't. If I just turn up, she might not realize how late it really is. Especially if Jon's with me— and some of the other actors too, with a bit of luck.

"Okay, you've persuaded me. You'll wait for me to get changed, won't you?"

"I already said I would. Off you go, and I'll go find the others and call a cab. Meet us in the parking lot."

He leans forward and gives me a kiss on the cheek. I think I've died and gone to heaven. I give a huge, dozy smile and run off, hoping he doesn't notice I've gone bright red.

. . .

"Dance?" Jon whispers in my ear, sending shivers shooting up and down my spine.

"Sure." I take a long slurp of my drink through the straw and get up. Then promptly fall back down again. "Ooops." I giggle.

Jon takes my hand and guides me up from my chair. "Allow me," he says.

He keeps hold of my hand as we head towards the dance floor, and it's so exciting because, as we walk, the crowds of people part to let us through. They know we're part of the movie crowd.

This club is insane. And I got in without being carded. There are low round tables with stools around them, and there's actually a waterfall beside the bar. Liv will be so jealous when I tell her. The owner of the club has been sending over cocktails for us all night—free. I think he's angling for a visit to the set so he can meet Tilly. He certainly keeps talking about her enough, asking where she is and if she'll be coming by later. Jon's being all noncommittal, saying that he's not sure, but she could be. I guess he doesn't want to stop the drinks from coming.

"Hey," calls a voice next to me. "Want to come home with me tonight?"

"Sorry," drawls Jon. "She's with me."

My heart pounds in my chest. It's like I'm in the best fantasy ever.

"No problem," says the guy who, judging by his appearance, wouldn't look twice at me under normal circumstances. "What about an autograph instead?"

The people he's with laugh, and so does Jon. I'm in too much of a daze to do anything other than grin inanely.

"Later," Jon says.

We float to the dance floor. Okay, I'm the one doing

the floating, but what do you expect? I just hope this doesn't turn out to be a dream.

Someone's looking out for me tonight, because after we've been dancing for a very short while they play a slow song, and Jon wraps his arm around my waist and pulls me close. The smell of his cologne invades my senses. I don't know what it is, but I'll remember the smell for as long as I live.

"Having fun?" Jon asks.

What a question. How could I not be?

"Mmmm," I say.

"Better than some boring party?"

Oh, no. The party. I haven't been paying attention to the time since... What time is it? My arms are linked around Jon's neck, but I manage to press the light on my watch so I can see. Crap. It can't be.

It's past one.

Guilt shoots through me. I have to go. But Jon's the first guy I've really liked who's liked me back. Not counting relegated-to-the-Friend-Zone Matt, so I'm not thinking about him. Everything is so magical that I can't spoil it. But I have to. It's Liv's party, and I can't let her down.

"I have to go," I say softly, and he pulls his head back a little and gazes into my eyes.

Whoa. He's going to kiss me. I know he's going to kiss me—I've seen that look before. Only this time he'll be kissing me intentionally and not by mistake. What if he thinks I'm the most awful kisser he's ever known? I close my eyes and prepare myself for a memorable experience.

Suddenly, an elbow in my back makes me stumble, and I fall forward. Jon's grip tightens, keeping me from losing my balance.

I jerk my head around and a flash of light blinds me. My hands instinctively shield my eyes. What the…

"Get out of here," Jon growls. He pushes the guy with the camera aside, pulls me by the arm, and marches off the dance floor. I wish he wouldn't squeeze my arm so hard. It's really hurting.

We get back to our table, and Jon sort of gently pushes me down on the seat. I slide along to make room for him to sit, but he just stands there a frown on his face.

"What's wrong?" I ask.

"Nothing. I'm just going to talk to someone, I'll be back in a minute."

"But the party. I have to…"

"I won't be long," he says, interrupting me and leaning down and resting his arm on my shoulder. "I'll stop at the bar and ask them to send over another cocktail for you. Okay?" He walks away before I have time to answer.

I lean back and close my eyes, but quickly open them again since having them closed makes me feel sick. What's so important that he has to leave me on my own? I wonder where Vince is. I haven't seen him, or the others, for a long time. We all sat together at first, but one by one they all disappeared. He might be with the girl from craft services. They always seem to be together these days. She's really nice. I hope something happens between them.

"Hey, Abi. You okay?"

Well, how spooky is that? I think about Vince, and he appears. "Sure. Seat?" I pat the bench beside me.

Just as he's sitting the bartender arrives with my cocktail, which he places in front of me. I pick it up and take a long drink.

"Don't you think you've had enough?" Vince asks.

Excuse me. Who does he think he is, my mother? "I can handle my liquor, you know." I glare at him.

"You could have fooled me. I saw you staggering all over the dance floor."

"That's not true. Some photographer guy blinded me with his flash, and I lost my balance."

"Yeah, right. Come on, Abi. Don't do anything you'll regret in the morning."

"What's that supposed to mean?"

"With Jon. You might be Tilly on the set, but you're not her. Remember that."

"Look, if all you're going to do is lecture me, then go away, thank you very much." I pointedly pick up my glass and drink the rest of it straight down.

Ooops. I don't think that was such a good idea. I

can feel it bubbling in the pit of my stomach. Oh, God, please don't let me vomit. Not here, it would spoil everything.

I draw in a long deep breath, which stems the feeling a little.

"I'm not trying to be your mother. But I do care about you. You're a good kid, and I don't want to see you get hurt."

Kid. He's calling me a kid. Is that what they all think of me? Is that how Jon sees me?

I'm not a kid. I'm eighteen. I'm not much younger than Tilly. How come they don't think of her as a kid? You'd think it would have been harder for her to be taken seriously as an adult since she grew up in the entertainment industry. Maybe that's why she's so prickly all of the time. Right now, I can hardly blame her.

"I won't get hurt, and I'm not naïve either. I know things." I cross my arms and scowl at him.

"Yes, I can see that." Vince shakes his head. "Come on, why don't I get you home?"

"Move it, Vince." Jon's voice makes me start. "I want to sit next to Abi."

"Abi and I were just leaving. She's ready to go."

I am? I didn't say that. And I wouldn't. Why would I spoil such an awesome night by going home? Ridiculous.

Jon looks from Vince to me. "You are?"

Sorry, Vince, but opportunities like this don't come along very often. If at all. "Of course not. The evening's barely begun." I fix my eyes firmly on Jon, not daring to look at Vince.

"But…" says Vince.

"Don't worry about me, Vince. I'll be fine. You go." I give a dismissive wave.

"What about your friend's party?" He arches an eyebrow.

"First you want me to go home. Now you want to go to the party. What is it with you?" I'm getting fed up of him interfering. I can look after myself.

"Forget it." Vince holds up both his hands. "Do what you want, I'm off. See you Monday." He gets up and walks away without even looking back.

Now I feel like crap. But I'll get over it now that Jon's back, and we can be together.

"Was that your phone?" Jon says interrupting my thoughts.

"What? I don't know. I didn't hear anything. I'll check." I reach into my purse and pull it out. It's a text from Liv: *How could you? I hope it's worth it. DON'T reply. EVER.*

Chapter Fourteen

My head really hurts. As in, there's-a-herd-of-elephants-charging-through-my-brain really hurts. If I never see a pink cocktail again, it will be way too soon.

I pull the pillow over my face to shield myself from the light shining through the gap at the bottom of the drapes, which is making me feel even worse. If that's possible.

I've never been so wasted in my whole life. Not that I make a habit of drinking excessively. Not ever, really. Usually a couple of beers at a party and that's about it. I always have to think about my training and keeping fit, so I can't go crazy. Not that Matt or Liv would let me get in that state, even if I wanted to.

What's even scarier is I don't remember coming

home last night. Well, that's not altogether true. I do have a vague recollection of Jon putting me in a cab, giving me a quick kiss on the cheek, and giving the driver some money. The rest is sort of a mystery.

Mom's going to freak. I can only hope she was in bed when I got back and that I used the key under the flowerpot around the back of the house to let myself in and that I was quiet.

Oh, God. Liv.

Her party. Her text. Oh, no.

I felt bad before, but suddenly it's reaching new lows.

Why didn't I go to the party last night?

Why did I allow myself to be persuaded to go to The Tavern?

Why did I spend such a wonderful evening with Jon?

That's the only question I can answer. Jon definitely would have full on kissed me if we hadn't been interrupted by that freakin' photographer. I've never been this crazy this quickly about a guy before. We get along so well. He's so kind and thoughtful, and look how he stayed with me all evening. He's never said anything about my stutter. Not that I've really stuttered that much in front of him. I seem to save that up for when I'm with Tilly. And what a nice guy he is for putting me in a cab home. He didn't try and take advantage of me being wasted. That says a lot about him.

I know I keep saying this, but why can't Jon be with me instead of Tilly? It's not like she really wants him.

It's all for publicity. That's what Vince said. To promote her image. So all her fans think she's a nice girl and not some slut. I wish he could see her as she really is, and then he might try to do something about it. He just doesn't deserve to be treated the way she treats him. He should be with someone who'll be there when he needs them. Someone who won't put themselves first all the time. Someone like me.

Liv will understand. She's got to. It's not like I'm the life and soul of the party, so she couldn't have really missed me. She probably sent that text after she'd had a few. She might not even remember. I'll call her later, once I've gotten up. Maybe go over to her place. She hasn't even seen my present yet. Thanks to earning all this money, I was able to get her this beautiful silver bangle, and I had it engraved on the back so she always thinks of me when she wears it.

A loud knock on the door sets off the pounding in my head again, which had subsided a little.

"Abi, sweetheart. Are you awake?"

It's Mom. She doesn't sound angry, which is definitely promising. "Yeah," I mutter, from under the pillow.

I hear the door open and the sound of her footsteps as she pads across my floor. The bed bounces when she sits down beside me, and I feel decidedly nauseous. She better keep still, or I'll be in serious need of a huge bucket.

"I didn't realize you were coming home last night," she says, way too loud for my liking. Doesn't she know how to whisper? "I was very surprised to see your shoes and purse in the hall when I got up this morning. How was Liv's party?"

At least I didn't wake her. That's good. Now let's see how she takes what I'm about to say next.

"I didn't go to the party," I say, lifting up the pillow slightly and speaking from under it.

"You didn't go to the party?" Mom says, her voice about an octave higher. "But you phoned and said you were going straight from work. What do you mean you didn't go to the party? Where did you go?" She grabs hold of the pillow and yanks it off my head.

I cover my eyes with my arm. "I'm sorry. I meant to, but it got late. I went out with the guys from work to a club, and they brought me home in a cab." That sounds so lame. Because it is.

"And missed your best friend's party? Oh, Abi. How could you?" She glares at me, her eyes tiny, disappointed slits.

You'd think I'd committed a heinous crime. It's only a party, for heaven's sake. She's just trying to make me feel guilty. And it's working. Guilt floods through me, spoiling my memories of last night.

"Liv will understand," I say without conviction. Because I'm not really sure she will.

"Are you sure about that?" My eyes are now closed,

but I can feel her stony gaze penetrating my arm, which is resting across my head. "And of course, if she did the same thing to you, you wouldn't mind, would you?"

Shut up. Shut up. Shut up. I've got the message. I'm the worst friend in history.

Why doesn't she go downstairs and do some cooking, or cleaning, or some other motherly thing she does with her time? Anything, just leave me alone.

"Don't start, Mom. I don't feel well."

"Well, don't expect me to be sympathetic. You shouldn't even be drinking at your age, and especially not drinking so much you have a hangover."

"Whatever." The word is out my mouth before I have time to check it. I know what the reaction's going to be.

"Don't you *whatever* me. I suggest you get out of bed now and call Liv to apologize."

She practically leaps off the bed, causing me to bounce so much that bile shoots up from my stomach into my mouth, then she stomps out of my room and slams the door behind her, not bothering to wait for my reply.

Mom's so annoying. Where does she get off, ordering me out of bed?

. . .

I take a bite of the tuna and mayo sandwich Mom left

on the kitchen table for me. The thought of eating it is turning my stomach, but she'll only get onto me again if I don't try to manage some of it.

"Ah, the *movie star* has arisen," Dad says walking into the kitchen and pulling out the chair at the end of the table and sitting down.

"Very funny," I say.

"It wasn't supposed to be. Your mother told me about last night, and I'm not impressed." He fixes me with one of his stares that used to terrify me when I was about six. Now, I know better.

"I didn't mean to. It just sort of happened. I'm going to phone Liv and say sorry." If she'll speak to me. Before I came down, I re-read the text from last night. I don't remember it being that bad.

"Good. In the future, I don't want you to go out with the movie crowd." He thumps the table, and the little white china salt and pepper pots in the middle jump up and down.

What's gotten into him? It's not like I've been arrested for drugs. All I did was have a few drinks and miss a party. I think he's getting a bit carried away.

"But…"

"No buts, Abi. Have you seen today's paper?" I shake my head. "I thought not. Just look at this." He leans over to the middle of the table and pulls the newspaper toward him. "What do you have to say for yourself?" He stabs his finger at a photo and then slides it across to where I'm sitting.

It's a picture of me with my hair plastered across my face, with the caption *Movie Mess*. My eyes are almost crossed, and I'm being held up by Jon. I look like a freakin' wreck. I lean forward and rest my head in my hand. How can this be happening to me? At least my name isn't in print, because they didn't know who I was. I glance up at Dad who's glaring at me. "Oh," I say.

"Oh. Is that it?" Dad snaps. "How much did you have to drink for God's sake? Not to mention you're underage and could've got into a lot of trouble. Or doesn't that matter in your world?"

I've never seen Dad so angry. But I don't know why. It's not like he didn't drink when he was my age, because he did. He's told me.

"I didn't drink much. It's just that there wasn't time to eat. That's why it affected me." My voice cracks, much to my annoyance.

Mom walks into the kitchen, and I can tell by the look on her face it's her turn now.

"So, what do you have to say for yourself?" She folds her arm tightly across her chest.

"Nothing. It's worse than it looks." I pause. "I mean it's not as bad as it looks. I slipped. That's why Jon's holding me up. I didn't drink that much, but it went to my head because I forgot to eat."

I don't know why I'm making excuses to them. It's not gonna change anything.

"Who's Jon?"

"Tilly's boyfriend."

"And where was Tilly when he was holding you up so inelegantly?" Mom asks.

"She was sick and stayed at the hotel."

"All on her own with no one to look after her, I suppose," Mom said shaking her head from side to side. Typical of Mom to think of that.

"She can look after herself."

"Hmm. That's debatable. She's not much older than you."

"Well, I can look after myself, too. If you'd let me." My head still hurts, and arguing is making it worse.

"Well, it doesn't look that way in the photo, and that's what the world is going to see. You're not to go out with those people again."

"But, I…"

My cell ringing interrupts me, and I snatch it up, happy for some relief from the cross examination.

"It's Matt," a voice says. I stand up and walk out the kitchen, closing the door behind me. I don't want Mom and Dad listening to what I know is going to be a difficult conversation.

"H-h-hello."

"Man, you've outdone yourself this time," Matt's voice booms in my ear, and I wince.

"I'm *so* sorry. I couldn't help it…"

"Cut the crap, Abi. You've made it perfectly clear

who comes first in your world, and we know it's not us."

Ouch.

"No. No. That's so not true. Please Matt. I got drunk, and the time just passed, and I really wanted to go to the party. I know Liv's going to hate me. I'll call her to explain."

"And you think that's going to fix everything, do you?"

No. But how can I admit that? I'd kill for a do-over. I'd make sure none of this happened. "She'll understand. I know she will." I force my voice to sound confident, but I don't know why, because it's not like I can fool Matt.

"God Abi. If it wasn't for her, you wouldn't have even done this stupid movie. And this is how you thank her."

"Okay, okay. I hear you. I know Liv has every right to hate me forever, and I understand if she doesn't want to speak to me again. But I'm sorry. I really am. I'll make it up to you both. Promise."

"We'll see." He's silent for a few seconds. "I better go. I'll see you soon."

"I hope so, too. But we're so behind, Zac was talking about us staying really late from now on." *Shut up. That isn't the right thing to say.*

"Sure."

The sound of Matt ending the call echoes in my ear.

Chapter Fifteen

"Abi, upstairs. My office," Bill growls during a break while we're teaching the junior's class, fixing me with one of his don't-mess-with-me stares.

Which is just great. What does *he* want? Surely it's not because I was five minutes late? I mean, it wasn't like they'd already started warming up by the time I got here. When I arrived, Bill was giving his usual lecture about the championships, and, to be honest, I've heard his talk so many times before I could do it for him. *And* I'm doing him a favor by helping out because he's short trainers. Anyway, he's lucky I made it at all. I nearly didn't, because Zac was on the verge of re-shooting a whole scene, until it started to rain.

So, Bill better be careful, because if he gets on my

case, then I'm going to walk. I really don't need this at the moment. On top of everything with Liv, I finish shooting the day after tomorrow, and I'm dreading it, because it means I'm going to lose all my new friends. My *only* friends after what happened with Liv.

And let's not even think about how things are with Jon. He's hardly spoken to me since our night at the club. Not because he's ignoring me, but for some reason Tilly's sticking to him like glue. As soon as we start to talk she appears, as if by magic. I swear she's got some sort of tracking device on him. When he goes back to L.A. with her… I just can't bear to think about it.

"Okay," I finally say, after Bill gives a loud cough.

I walk up the stairs behind him, dragging my feet for good measure. Not that he seems to notice my annoyance, or, if he does, he chooses to ignore it.

When we get to his office, he closes the door behind us, walks to the desk, and leans against it with his arms folded.

"Care to explain?" he asks, fixing me with a stare.

"What?" I can't bring myself to keep eye contact with him, so I look down at my feet instead.

"Your attitude. You used to be a good role model for the younger ones, but now you act like being here is something you *have* to do and not something you *want* to do. I don't like it. I hope you'll be back to your old self when you resume training. Nationals will be upon us before we know it, and you'll be lucky to qualify let alone make it to the finals."

Excuse me? How dare he get on my case when he was the one who made me go for the movie job in the first place? If anything, he should be building me up, not trying to bring me down.

"I'm sorry. But the movie…"

"Isn't your whole life, and filming will be over very soon. Then you'll be back here with us."

That's what I'm dreading. How can I come back here where class is boring and I'd much rather be with the people from the movie? Plus, I don't even know if I want to continue with class. There are so many other things I can do. Like…like…travel to L.A. and take up stunt work professionally. All I've ever done is kickboxing, and, thanks to the movie, I know there's more to life than that. I don't want to upset Bill, though. I owe him big time. I know that, but people move on. I'm moving on. It's not his fault that my life is changing direction, so I shouldn't take it out on him or everyone here. I get that.

"I promise to be enthusiastic with the juniors when I'm here and to make sure I'm on time." Hopefully that will keep him off my back for a while. Then, once I'm back here and have time to plan my future, I'll talk to him.

"Thank you." An expression of relief crosses his face, which makes me feel bad. He needs me more than I thought. "I know you've got a lot on your plate.

But don't alienate everyone." I think he's getting a bit carried away. The only person who I've had a falling out with is Liv, which I admit was my fault. Other than that, there's no one else I've *alienated*. Well, there's Matt too, I guess, which feels too awful to think about, so I push it out out of my head before I can overanalyze it. But that's it. I'm the same as I've always been, apart from being busier and having more friends.

"Sure. Thanks. Can I go now?" Bill nods.

I race downstairs to look for Matt but don't see him anywhere. It's so annoying. It's not like there are loads of places to go. Unless he's deliberately keeping out of my way. We haven't seen each other since he cut short our call the other day, but we have exchanged a few texts. So there's no reason for him to totally ignore me.

After a few more minutes looking for Matt, I decide to go outside for a while until class starts again. While I'm leaning against the wall, I spot him walking along the sidewalk. Where's he been? There aren't any shops around here. It's all industrial. Maybe he has been avoiding me, after all.

"Hey, Matt," I shout, striding toward him. He glances up but doesn't acknowledge me or anything.

"You managed to make it tonight, then," he says when I reach him.

"Don't you start. I've just had an earful from Bill. And I explained everything to him. Anyway, it's not my fault filming ran over."

Even I'm feeling that this excuse is wearing thin.

"It never is." He looks down at the ground, his happy, flirty Matt energy nowhere to be found.

It's so not fair that I have to spend my time defending what I do. My entire life it's been: *Abi, push yourself more; Abi, don't let people walk all over you; Abi, stand up for yourself; Abi, don't hide from the limelight.* Need I go on? And now—NOW—all I get is abuse for doing the very thing everyone wanted me to do in the first place.

"Filming finishes in a couple of days, so that should make you all happy." I give a hollow laugh. "Back to my boring existence. Or should I say boring *non-existence.*"

"If that's what you think of me and Liv."

That's not fair. I didn't say that. He's just twisting it to make me feel guilty. "Liv's not speaking to me, despite all my efforts to contact her, and all you can do is complain. What do you expect me to think? It's hardly something to look forward to, is it?"

"Whose fault is that?" He folds his arms across his chest and fixes me with an accusatory stare.

I can't believe I'm standing here listening to this. How dare he? I've been the best friend to him and Liv. I've listened to them go on and on about their parents and brothers and sisters. Supported anything they've done, like when Matt made the football team. Been there when things have gone wrong. And now, just because my life is different and for once I'm having fun, they're both being total jerks about it.

"Forget it. Just forget it. You're deliberately taking everything I say the wrong way." I wave my arms in the air, out of temper. "I take it Liv still isn't acknowledging my existence."

"Do you blame her?" His fists are balled, and he punches one into his thigh.

I swallow hard. I hate when we fight. "But I didn't mean to. It just happened."

"That's just a cop out, if you ask me."

"So sue me," I snap. Then guilt floods through me. Because it is all my fault. "I want to speak to Liv. To say sorry. But how can I if she won't take my calls or reply to my texts?"

"Just give her time. She'll calm down eventually. You know what she's like," Matt says, sounding more like his usual self.

"Do you know that for sure, or are you just assuming? Have you talked about it?"

"Not really," he says, a guilty expression crossing his face.

Yeah, right, they haven't mentioned me at all. If he expects me to believe that then he's lost it. I bet she said something really hateful, and he doesn't want to tell me in case I go off at him.

"The truth, Matt." I give him my best intimidating glare, but all it does is make him roll his eyes. Okay, maybe I'm not cut out for acting, and maybe I'm overreacting a little.

"She's still upset," he says gently. "Give her time. I haven't seen her since the party either. She's been spending so much time with Rich."

"Liv got together with Rich? Did it happen at the party? Why didn't you tell me?" I lock eyes with Matt, and he shuffles his feet. His cheeks have a faint pink tinge, and he looks decidedly awkward. "Well?" I demand.

"She asked me not to," Matt mutters.

"She *what*?" I can't believe she'd do that. So much for me overreacting. What about her? "Fine. Well, I won't tell her what happened with Jon, then."

"Jon, as in the guy who goes out with Tilly?" He frowns.

Darn. Now he's going to give me the twenty questions and no doubt tell me Jon's too old for me, or he's already with someone, or whatever sensible thing he'll think of. Matt's nothing if not sensible. Not that it's bothered me before, but, as I keep saying, things aren't like they were before.

"Yes."

"What about him? You're not…"

"No," I say, shaking my head. "Not yet, but we had a great time together at the club. I planned to explain all this to Liv, because that's part of why I missed her party. But no point now, is there?"

"And you figure he'll go out with you rather than

Tilly? You're kidding, right?"

"You don't understand. Tilly doesn't want him. It's just a game to her. You should only know half of what she's done to him."

The strangest expression crosses Matt's face, but I can't work out what it means.

"And he puts up with it?"

"I'm not sure how much he knows. I wanted to say something, but Vince said not to."

"Well, at least someone is thinking straight."

"Meaning?" I frown.

"Vince. And you need to start, too. You should be staying out of this sort of thing. You know what these celebs are like."

"Actually, I do, and I don't think I should stay out of it, as you say. The only reason Jon stays with Tilly is because he feels sorry for her. He says underneath it all she's really insecure."

"She doesn't sound like it to me."

"That's because she's a good actor."

"Anyway, isn't Tilly your all-time hero, in which case how can you even think about taking away her boyfriend?"

"It's not like that. You don't understand. All you want to do is ruin everything for me." My voice gets louder by the syllable.

Why doesn't he understand?

Why doesn't anyone understand?

. . .

"Abi, we're going to Rosie's Bar, you coming?" Vince asks.

I'd planned on going around to Liv's house to see if I can persuade her to talk to me, but what's the point? She knows I'm sorry. I've left enough texts and messages for her, which she hasn't answered. And since going home isn't exactly an exciting prospect, I might as well hang out with people who like me.

"Sure, I'll meet you there in fifteen. It won't take me long to clean up."

Listen to me. It wasn't that long ago when I'd have gone through all sorts of mental torture at the thought of going out with a group of people. Especially to a bar. Not that I'd have gone into a bar in the past, seeing as we're not old enough. Now, I'm okay with it. Sort of.

Fifteen minutes somehow turns into thirty, and as I make my way to Rosie's, I end up getting caught in a rain shower.

I head for the bathroom when I get there. While I'm patting myself down with a paper towel, the door swings open and in staggers Tilly, her complexion a delicate shade of green and her eyes all glazed.

"Tilly, you look awful. Are you okay?" I rush over to her. I'm probably asking for a verbal smackdown, but I can't help it. I can't just leave her when she looks like a tabloid horror story waiting to happen.

"Shhhhhutup. Thersh nothing wrong with me." She stumbles, and I manage to catch her under the arms before she hits the floor.

"Come and sit down," I say, leading her toward the black leather sofa.

"Get off me." She pulls away and starts to wobble, so I grab hold of her arm again. "I feel sick," she moans.

This is so weird, me taking care of Tilly.

"Okay, let's go into a stall." I kick open the stall door, and we both squeeze in.

She leans forward, and I just manage to pull her hair out of the way in time before she vomits into the toilet.

The smell is so disgusting that I think I might join her. And let's not even think about the bit that's splattered over my shoes.

We stay in this position for what seems like forever. Luckily, no one comes into the bathroom.

Finally, when she's all vomited out, Tilly stands. I take her by the arm and sit her down on the sofa. I get some wet paper towels and gently mop her face. She still doesn't look too good. I hope she's not gonna throw up again.

"How do you feel?" Hopefully better than she looks, though at least her face has gone from green to white. Her hair needs brushing. It's all over the place.

"I'm fine," Tilly mumbles. "You can leave me now."

I don't think I should. She might fall, bang her head, and knock herself out. Or worse. She could hit her head on the sink and then die. I can't leave her yet. Definitely not. "It's okay. I'll hang around for a while until you're feeling a bit better." I sit next to her and take one of the paper towels and wipe the mess off my shoes. At least it didn't stain, since these are my favorite.

"Whatever." Tilly shrugs.

"I won't tell anyone, if that's what you're worried about."

"I don't think that would make a difference, the sort of reputation I have." She gives a wry smile.

"Why do it then?" The question the media would pay mega-bucks for an answer to, no doubt.

"No reason. Apart from I can. All my life I've been able to do what I want. And then my management complains about me screwing-up my image. Well, they can't have it both ways. They can't give me the liquor and pills and then moan at what happens to me. I tell them it's to escape from the pressure of being a *big* star. Although, even that's debatable, if you read the press; they're calling me a 'has-been.' At my age. What a joke. A lonely has-been with no friends."

"You must have some friends?" I ask.

"Yeah, I do. Except I never know if they're with me for the fame or because they really like me. I can't trust any of them. They'd all let me down given half the chance and the offer of some money from the press."

Like I let down Liv.

It suddenly occurs to me I'm no better than all

these so called friends of Tilly's. All the time I've been thinking of myself. What I want, and how Liv and Matt didn't understand. Maybe I should've thought more about how my actions affected them.

"Well, you can trust Jon. He's on your side."

"Jon's on no one's side but his own." Her lip curls up in a sneer.

"But he's always looking out for you?"

"If you say so."

"Is that why you cheat on him?" I have to ask, and hope she doesn't take it the wrong way.

"Maybe." She shrugs.

"Well, at least you have your mom," I say, instantly regretting my words after remembering what I witnessed down by the river.

"You think?" Tears form in her eyes.

"I'm so sorry." I rest my hand on top of hers. "I didn't mean to upset you. I forget not all moms are like mine. My mom wants to meet you, by the way. She always says there's not much that her special chocolate muffins can't fix."

Tilly gives a hollow laugh. "Why would I want to hang out with you and your boring family? I'm not that desperate. I'm going back. I'm fed up sitting here."

Chapter Sixteen

Zac doesn't need me for the rest of the morning, so I'm doing some training to start getting back in shape. At the moment, I'm running around the lot. With shooting almost over, hopefully no one will mind. It's not like I'm going to be fighting and could injure myself, I'm just doing a workout. If I want any chance of doing well at Nationals after filming ends, then I need to improve my level of fitness.

Running past wardrobe, I accidentally knock into someone. "Sorry," I say. I glance up and see that it's Tilly.

Crap. I wait for the inevitable abuse. Why didn't I look where I was going instead of thinking about training?

"It's okay. I was in the way," Tilly replies, stepping to

the side and allowing me to pass.

My jaw drops. What's gotten into her? Where's the snarky comment? The one that trips off the end of her tongue so instinctively it's like she doesn't even have time to think about it. Ridiculous.

"Oh. See you later," I say, pulling myself together and then going from jogging in one spot to running again.

"Wait," Tilly calls.

I stop and glance back over my shoulder at Tilly, who's heading toward me. Since when does Tilly come to someone? It's always us going to her.

"Yes?" I ask when she gets close.

She looks at me from under her lashes and there's a pink tinge to her cheeks, like she's embarrassed or something. What the heck's going on? "I just want to say thanks," she says quietly.

My jaw drops, and I have the strongest urge to pinch myself to make sure I'm not in the middle of a weird dream. "Um...what for?"

"For helping me the other night in the bar." She shifts from foot to foot, looking uneasy.

"That's okay." All other words escape me.

"And sorry for being mean about your family."

Now she's just messing with me. She must be on something. She's never considered my feelings before.

"Okay." I stare hard at her face, trying to see some sign of her playing a joke, but she looks genuine enough.

Then again, she is an actress.

"I would like to meet your mom sometime. I love chocolate muffins."

My heart softens. She really is trying to make an effort with me. Of course, it would have helped if she'd done it sooner. Or is there some ulterior motive? Maybe she wants me to do something for her. Crap. I just don't know what to think. It would be great for us to be friends. Or just get along better.

"Yeah. Sure. Of course. We'll figure something out."

I'd love to tell Liv and Matt about this, but of course that's not gonna happen. They couldn't care less how Tilly treats me. Still, Vince will be interested. Although he thinks I'm too sensitive as far as Tilly is concerned. I admit she can be mean to everyone, but I still say that I get more than my fair share of her snark. A lot more. Vince hasn't hear the half of what's gone down.

"Abi."

The sound of my name cuts across my thoughts, and I stare in the direction of the voice and see Danny beckoning for me to come over. Please don't let him say he wants to rehearse tomorrow's scene again. We've gone over it so many times I'm even dreaming about it. I get that it's a big stunt scene, and it will be awesome when we actually shoot it, but sometimes if you practice something too much, it can lose its edge. It still needs to be fresh so the cameras can capture the moment. Well, that's what Vince says, and he should know.

"I better go," I say to Tilly and jog over to where Danny is standing.

"Hi," I say.

"I wanted to speak to you on your own," Danny says.

My body tenses. What have I done wrong now? And why do I have to be alone?

"O-okay," I say.

I draw in a deep breath and wait. Danny's a great guy, but he's really strict on set. He needs to be. For obvious reasons. And if there's something wrong, he makes sure you know about it. So it must be bad if he doesn't want to say it in front of the others.

"Relax, Abi." he says. "I'm not about to tear you a new one." He shakes his head, and I feel stupid for overreacting.

"Oh." I wrap my arms loosely around my middle and shift from foot to foot. I try to seem relaxed, but it's not easy, and I suspect I'm not managing it.

"You finish soon, and I was wondering what your plans are for the future."

I chew on the inside of my cheek. This is weird. Why does he want to know? And why does this conversation have to be between the two of us? He's never been interested in my future before.

"Um. Not sure yet. Mom made me apply to the local community college." And how lame does that make me sound. *Mom made me.* What about what I want?

"Have you thought of doing stunt work professionally?"

Have I? Yeah, of course. But that's in my dreams. "Sort of. But I can't afford to go to L.A. and try to find work." Not to mention I'm not ready to go anywhere on my own, however much I'd love to. Travelling is what I should be doing with Liv, or Matt. But the way things are between us, I can't guarantee it will ever happen. Liv might never speak to me again.

"You're a natural. I've never seen anyone take to stunt work so well on their first attempt. Really, you should think seriously about doing it. You've got your SAG card, and now you need to get an agent. I can put you in touch with a couple of good ones. And you can put my name on your resume."

I want to fling my arms around Danny and give him a big hug. I can't believe he'd do that. It's the nicest thing anyone has ever done for me.

"Really? You think I could do it?" I say, my voice sounding all breathless.

Could this day get any better? Tilly being cool with me. And now Danny offering to help get my career off the ground. It's better than anything I could've imagined. And having Jon being so lovely to me, too. It's like everything that happened to me over the last ten years is now behind me.

"I wouldn't support you if I didn't think so. I have a reputation to think about. Bill was right when he said how good you are. Such a quick learner, too." He pats me on the back.

Thanks, Bill. I owe him one. But I really can't do anything until after Nationals. It wouldn't be fair if I wasn't there to represent the dojo.

I rest my hand on my chest. "Thanks so much, Danny. I really appreciate it. And thanks for all your help on set. I couldn't have done it without you."

All the tension in my body disappears, and I feel warm, relaxed, and happy. I let out a contented sigh, and Danny chuckles. He probably thinks I'm silly, because for him it's not such a big deal, but at this precise moment I don't care.

"My pleasure, kid. I'll email you the agents' names for you to check out and choose one you like. Remember to say I recommended you. That will set you apart from the others they see. If I say so myself."

He walks away, and I stand there open-mouthed. I can't believe what just happened. I want to pinch myself to make sure I'm really awake and not having the most incredible dream. It looks like I could have something to look forward to in the future after all. But I can't help thinking how much better it would be if Matt and Liv could share it with me.

Chapter Seventeen

As soon as the scene wraps, I run to the craft services table. Jon caught me earlier between scenes and asked me to meet him there. I've no idea what for. He seemed very serious though.

When I get there, he's standing to the side of the table, leaning against the wall. A beaming smile crosses his face as he sees me heading toward him. That's so weird. It's so different from how he was before. Unless I misread his face. Or maybe because I was on set so he didn't want to disturb me too much. Whatever, it doesn't matter.

"Yes?" My voice doesn't sound like normal, more from the excitement of talking to Jon than exerting myself, I suspect.

"I need you."

What? He needs me. Does he mean needs me as in *needs me*? Is it over between him and Tilly? It would be like all my dreams coming true at the same time if he wants to take me back to L.A. with him.

"What for?" I look into his eyes. They seem troubled.

"It's Tilly," he says, shaking his head. I was right. "She's been on one of her benders." So that's why she hasn't shown her face yet today. "And tonight is the premiere of *Gaslight* in New York. She was supposed to be coming with me."

I can't wait to see Jon in the movie. It's a remake of the classic *Gaslight*, and it's set in London. Jon's the Inspector who solves the crime. He'll be perfect, and no one will be able to mock his accent, because he's supposed to be British.

"Oh no, what are you going to do?" I make myself sound concerned, even if I am jumping up and down with excitement on the inside. Not that I know what he wants me to do.

"That's where you come in." He rests his arm around my shoulder, and my heart does a triple flip. Or is it a quadruple flip? Whatever it is, my insides are definitely fizzing.

"Me?" I squeak. What is it with my freakin' voice? He'll think I'm so pathetic.

"You're to go home, pack a bag, and meet me at the

airport at two. We've got a private plane waiting to fly us to New York and bring us back tomorrow."

He wants me to go with him as his date. He's had enough of Tilly. He wants to show the world it's over between them and that he's found someone else.

"New York?"

"I want you to pretend to be Tilly tonight at the premiere and the party after." My hand flies up to cover my mouth. "Don't worry. I'll be with you."

Oh. He doesn't want *me* there. He wants me as *Tilly* there. So it's not over between them. But even if it isn't, helping him out means spending time with him. So, it's a good thing. Okay, so it's not quite what I wanted, but it's a step in the right direction. Except there's the obvious problem to deal with: how the hell can I be Tilly in front of millions of people? Someone's sure to find out.

"I... me? Um, I..." My ability to produce any form of coherent speech seems to have deserted me.

"Breathe," Jon says kindly. "It'll be fine."

He knows this how? And what is it with everyone always telling me to breathe? It's not like I'm gonna stop.

"Yes, but..."

"Cut the *yes buts*. Nothing can go wrong. They're expecting Tilly to be with me, and if she isn't there, the rumors will start again. Tilly knows what we're doing. I'll be with you, and so will Bryan." He's Tilly's manager.

Now I get it. He's doing it to help Tilly. To stop the

rumors about her drinking. I might keep saying it, but it's true, he's just too good for her. Of course I want to help him.

"People will guess. My voice sounds nothing like Tilly's."

Stop with the excuses, or he'll change his mind about taking you with him.

That's easier said than done.

"We're ahead of you already. We're going to say you've lost your voice. Got laryngitis. Then no one will expect you to speak. It'll work." He gazes into my eyes. "Don't you want to come with me?" Disappointment flashes across his face. How can he ask such a question? I'd go anywhere with him.

"Of course I do," I say in my best casual voice. "You know that."

"Cool."

"But, what about clothes? I don't have anything suitable, and what will I tell Mom and Dad? They might not want me to go, and…" My casual attitude transforms seamlessly into one of mad panic.

"Whoa," Jon says, holding up his hand. "Clothes are no problem. Go and find Fran. I talked to her about our plans, and she'll fix you up with a dress and some jewelry. Then get your fairy ears taken off, leaving the nose and wig, obviously, and ask them to re-do your makeup. Borrow some, so you can touch it up yourself later."

"Okay." I nod my head deliberately, while inside telling myself to stay calm.

"As for your parents. You're not a child. You can make your own decisions." He's right. And I can't have him thinking of me as a silly teenager who can't even blow her nose without her parents' permission. That's hardly going to make him want to be with me in the future.

"Yes, sorry."

"But don't tell anyone what we're doing. No one can know. We can't risk the media frenzy if anyone finds out. It would be a disaster. For everyone." He shakes his head.

"Okay."

"Go now, meet me later and…"

"But…"

"Remember what I said? No buts. Are you okay for money, or do you need some for the cab?"

But…what I want to say is if I go now, I won't get to say good-bye to everyone. Today is the last day of filming. Vince mentioned a cast party this weekend, but I'm not sure when and where. What if they forget to invite me? Or what if they get annoyed that I disappeared without telling them and deliberately don't invite me?

Nothing's ever easy. I'll just have to text Vince and hope he understands. He can tell the others.

"I'm all good, thanks. I'll see you at two." I smile and

am rewarded with a to-die-for wink.

I half run and half walk away from him toward wardrobe. Actually, it's more like a skip. I can't wait to spend more time with Jon. Just the two of us.

. . .

Matt pulls up outside our house, and I run down the driveway to meet him.

"Thanks so much for taking me," I say, jumping in beside him.

He stares at me, frowning. "Why on earth are you dressed like that?"

I know Jon said not to mention it to anyone, but I can hardly keep it a secret from Matt, seeing as he's taking me to the airport. To be honest, I didn't think he'd agree when I called. Asking him was my last resort, since if I use my money for the cab fare it will wipe me out until I can get to the ATM. Well, not actually last resort—that would've been Mom. She's at work at the moment, and I didn't want to say anything. I've left a note for when she gets back. And I've got the credit card my Mom gave me for emergencies, so that will keep her happy.

"You have to promise not to say anything, because it's a secret." I lean in toward him and hold my finger up to my lips.

He shrugs. "Don't tell me then."

"I want to tell you. All I'm saying is you can't tell anyone."

If Liv was here I'd tell her, too. Maybe one day, if she ever forgives me, we can talk about it.

"Whatever." He turns to face the windshield and turns on the engine.

He's so frustrating. Most people would be dying to know. Then again, he's probably being like this because he knows I'm going to tell him anyway.

"I'm going to New York to Jon's movie premiere. Tilly's not well, so I'm pretending to be her."

He stops the engine and looks directly at me, scrutinizing my face. So much so I can feel heat rushing up my cheeks.

"Well, I suppose you could pass as Tilly. To those who don't know you well. But it seems crazy. Why can't they just say she couldn't make it?" He finally says.

"It's Jon's movie, and he wants her there."

"Why?"

Trust Matt to ask that. I hadn't even wondered. Just went along with it.

"It looks better to have a big star there, I guess."

"So he's using her."

I get a sudden flashback to what Tilly said about Jon only thinking of himself. But I still don't buy it. I can only go by how he's been with me, and how I've seen him with Tilly and the others on set.

"No. It's not like that. He's not like that." I pick up

the edge of my shirt and start to fiddle with it. I know I'm right about Jon.

"So, who else is going?" Matt asks.

"Jon." My word hangs in the air, and I glance at Matt. His expression is unreadable. Even to me.

"Just Jon?" That's all he says, but he shoots me a sharp glance that says a whole lot more. If only I knew what.

"Tilly's manager will be there. I think that's it." I shrug and act like it's no big deal.

"What, no entourage?" His sarcastic tone isn't wasted on me. Nor is the pointed strumming of his fingers on the steering wheel.

"I wondered that, too. But I'm not sure. It's Jon's night."

"What did your mom and dad say?" He arches an eyebrow, his face set firm.

"I haven't told them. Well, I've left them a note saying I'm going to the premiere with all the guys from the movie, to give Jon some support. Not that I'm going as Tilly. Or that there's only three of us going."

"They won't be happy." He shakes his head.

"I don't care. They don't control my life." I mean what I say, though it doesn't sit too well. I've never lied to them in the past.

"Don't go," he whispers. He gently grips my shoulders, facing me. We stare at each other for a moment, then he drops his arms and turns away. "They're just using you."

He sounds really pissed.

What's it to him? He's never supported me during the movie, and this is just more of the same. He's jealous because all this good stuff is happening to me. Because his life is the same as it always has been.

"Stop trying to ruin everything for me," I snap.

"I'm not," he says quietly.

"Well, that's how I see it. I just want to have some fun. Is that such a crime? It's not like anyone's gonna get hurt."

Chapter Eighteen

"What do you think?" Jon asks after we've walked up the steps onto the plane and the steward greets us.

What do I think? It's freakin' wild. I've only flown a few times before and always coach. This whole private jet thing is, well, just insane.

"Love it." I reply, having no other words to describe it.

"Sit wherever you like. The crew will serve drinks and food once we've taken off. I'll be back in a minute. I just want a quick word with Bryan."

I watch him walk away, hoping he won't be long, so we can talk about tonight. My biggest fear is going down the red carpet and the cameras zooming in on me. Millions of people around the world watch these shows on TV. People are bound to spot that I'm not Tilly, however good my makeup is. I'll have to keep my head down and tuck myself into Jon while we're walking. What if I trip? The silver strappy Christian Louboutin shoes Fran gave me to wear are ridiculously high even if they are cute, and Liv would kill for them. Or what if my dress rips? Though why should it? It's just that I remember a few years ago when the top of the dress of some presenter fell down and her bra was on show for the whole world to see. It was headline news.

"Hey, you okay?' Jon's voice drags me out of my nightmare scenario thoughts.

"Yeah, sure." I flash a bright smile. Maybe too bright. I just don't want him to think he's made a mistake by asking me.

"You didn't look it a moment ago," he says as he lowers himself into the seat next to me. He leans across and takes hold of my hand, and my heart skips a beat.

"Just thinking about tonight," I say, loving the warm feeling that's coursing through my veins at the moment.

"Don't worry, you'll be good. Before we leave for the premiere, I'll give you something that will help you relax."

If he means drugs, forget it. No way will I take any. No drugs. No cigarettes. I've always promised Mom and Dad, not that I've even been tempted. Not after a girl at school died from taking some illegal stuff.

"I'll be fine, really I will."

"Don't look so scared. It's your choice." He gives my hand a squeeze, and a shiver of excitement runs up my spine, causing me to squirm. I quickly turn it into a wriggle to make him think I'm trying to get comfortable.

"W-w-what would have happened if you'd gone without Tilly?" Even though I don't agree, I can't stop thinking about Matt's comments about Jon using Tilly. If I ask Jon, then it won't be in the back of my mind all the time.

"Nothing. I just didn't want to let her fans down. Some of them line up for hours just to catch a glimpse of her. At least now they will get one, even if it is you." He puts his arm around my shoulder and gives me a hug.

All the tension disappears from my body, and I relax into him. I knew it. Jon *is* one of the good guys. It was just Matt making me have these doubts. I'll tell him when I get back. In the meantime, I'm going to sit back and enjoy everything. Because this is going to be the most magical night ever.

. . .

WOW. And a million times WOW. My hotel room is beyond anything I've seen in my whole life, apart from in the movies. It's freakin' ginormous, and all I've been in so far is the lounge.

There's this huge bay window that opens up onto a balcony and goes all along one side of the room, giving an amazing view. It's dark outside, and the skyline is dotted with thousands of lights.

In the center of the lounge are two long sofas in a sort of wheat color, with rust-colored silk cushions. And along the wall is a dark wood sideboard with glass doors, and then there's a matching coffee table with a huge crystal bowl on top that's full of fruit.

I'm just about to sit down when I remember my dress needs hanging up. Jon said I should get the hotel to press it for me, but I figure it will be okay if I hang it.

I pick up my case and go into the bedroom. My jaw drops. It has a four-poster bed that's twice the size of my bed at home. No wonder Tilly gets all upset if she doesn't have the best of everything, if this is what she's used to.

After unzipping my case, I hang the dress up on the outside of the closet. It is a gorgeous, deep red long shift with a split all the way up one side that nearly hits my butt. Luckily, the straps are fairly wide, because of my false boobs. I gaze at the dress lovingly for a moment before heading into the bathroom with my toiletries bag.

The sound of a phone ringing interrupts my romantic dreams, and I scramble back to the bedroom and pick up the handset by the side of the bed.

"Hello?"

"Meet me in twenty minutes, downstairs in the bar," Jon says.

"But I thought you were going to come get me."

"I'm in the bar already. Pointless for me to go all the way up to the top again." Did I mention this is a penthouse suite?

"Sure. Where's the bar?" I have no desire, whatsoever, to walk into a crowded bar on my own looking like Tilly. I could get mobbed or anything. Surely Jon realizes this.

"To the left of the reception."

"Well, meet me in reception. If I'm supposed to be Tilly, people won't expect me to wander around on my own, will they?"

"Good point. But don't keep me waiting."

"I won't. Promise."

I replace the handset feeling happy with myself for actually standing up to Jon and letting him know what I want. Then I quickly call Mom and let her know I'm fine. She's a bit cranky with me for just leaving a note, but she'll get over it. I don't have time to get into a full-scale debate about it, anyway.

I then rush back to the bathroom so I can touch up my makeup. The stuff they use on set lasts forever, so it really is just a case of adding more lipstick and a touch of mascara.

As I stare at myself in the mirror, it hits me how used to seeing myself as Tilly I've become. I like what I see. It's cool looking like her. And it's not a shock now. In fact, sometimes seeing the real me makes me look twice.

Everything's going to be so strange now that I've

finished the movie, and I'm not sure I want to go back to how things were before, even if it is only for a short while until I get my career off the ground.

It's not that I wasn't happy. I was, sort of. But hanging out with Matt and Liv was never like this. However scared I am, it's going to be the most memorable time of my life.

I mentally crush the little voice of doubt that starts to rear up inside my head.

Chapter Nineteen

My heart's hammering like crazy against my rib cage. I don't think I can do this. Hundreds of people are lining the sides of the red carpet, behind rope barriers, shouting and screaming. And there are loads of cameras and reporters standing there with mics. I think I'm going to be sick, and that's no joke.

"Ouch," I cry out, as I feel a pinch on the side of my leg. Did Jon do that on purpose? Because it wasn't very nice.

"Hurry up, and be quiet," he says, in a loud whisper.

Yes, I think he did. Why?

The door of the black limousine we're in is being held open by our driver, but it's not like anyone would have heard me speak, not with all the noise going on out there.

I slide along the back seat and swing my legs around onto the pavement, trying to hold the sides of my dress together in the process so I don't give everyone an eyeful. Tilly probably wouldn't care if she gave everyone a glimpse of her booty, but I do. Bryan offers his hand as I get out. He must have left before us if he's already here.

As I stand upright, there's a huge eruption of screams. They must be for me. Well, Tilly-me, obviously. It's crazy. And exhilarating at the same time.

"Smile and wave," Bryan says without even moving his lips. "The way we practiced."

Just as I'm doing as Bryan tells me, Jon takes hold of my other arm and we walk slowly along the red carpet. Luckily I have Jon to lean on, because the noise and flashing cameras are making me feel dizzy, even through the sunglasses Jon brought for me to make sure that I would be taken for Tilly.

I give the Tilly wave and tilt my head to the side with the ironic smirk, just like she does and how I've practiced hundreds of times in the mirror.

"Hey Tilly, tell us about your new movie," yells one of the reporters as we pass.

"Ignore them," Jon whispers tersely in my ear.

I glare at him through my giant black lenses. Surely he doesn't think I'm going to speak to them? I'm not stupid.

Suddenly, I realize that I'm overreacting. I'm sure he didn't mean to get on my case. He's just nervous about the premiere. And worried about me being Tilly. I glance up at him and smile, trying to say sorry with my expression. I'm not sure if he understands, but he smiles back.

After what seems like forever, we get to the entrance of the movie theater, and as the doors close behind us, the silence hits me. Well, not total silence, but compared to what I've just been through…

"Well done," Jon says.

I nod, unsure whether I'm allowed to say anything yet. There aren't many people close by, but I don't want to risk upsetting Jon. Even though it's not super bright inside the theater, I keep the glasses on. Movie stars do that sometimes, right?

"Hi, I'm Dana," a young girl in uniform says as she walks up to us. "I'm here to show you to your seats." She looks directly at me. "I love your movies," she adds, lowering her voice a little.

I can't do anything but smile. She must think I'm so lame. Fortunately, Jon speaks.

"Thank you, that means a lot to Tilly." He puts his arm protectively around my shoulder and a shiver shoots down my spine. "She's got laryngitis. Doctor's orders to rest her voice."

I mouth, "Thank you."

"Poor you," says Dana. "Can I get you anything?"

I shake my head and give another smile, which causes her to lower her eyes and blush. I've never had that effect on anyone before. You know, in a different time and place, I could grow to enjoy this.

We follow her, and I just know all eyes are on me as I'm walking. It's the way pockets of silence precede my every step—people are talking, then see it's me, then stop and stare. I'm not imagining it. Inside I'm counting slowly and taking long breaths. I can't blush because, if I do, it will ruin everything. Tilly would never blush.

We walk through the double doors and into the gold section of the theater that has individual reclining seats. Dana stops by two seats at the end of a row and gestures with her arm for us to sit down. Bryan nods to Jon and then disappears. So it looks like it's just me and Jon together for the whole movie.

• • •

"You were amazing," I say to Jon when we're back in the limo and on the way to the party. "Your best movie so far."

I mean it. He was awesome. I couldn't take my eyes off him every time he was on screen.

"Thanks," he says, seeming more preoccupied with checking his messages than talking to me.

"Especially when you arrested Gregory. I was on the edge of my seat."

"Thanks," he mutters. "But I wasn't happy with the editing on that shot. They got my bad side."

"Well, I thought it was good," I reply, unsure what to say. There was no need for him to be rude to me. Then again, Vince told me that actors are always hyper-critical of themselves on screen, so it's probably that. "How long do we have to stay at the party?" I ask changing the subject.

I'm not looking forward to it. Having to stand in silence and have every move I make scrutinized by everyone. I'd much rather we went out for dinner somewhere and spent the rest of the night alone. We wouldn't have to talk about the movie, if Jon doesn't want to, which he will have to do while we're at the party.

"Not long," Jon replies, giving my leg a squeeze. "We're here," he adds glancing out of the window. "Now remember, not a word."

I grab the sunglasses that I'd put away in my purse for the ride and put them back on. "Got it," I say just as the driver opens the door.

"Ssshh," he hisses in my ear.

I'm just about to say sorry when luckily something inside makes me slap a mental hand over my mouth. Why didn't someone tell me this was going to be so hard? We're not even in the party yet.

I link my arm through his, and we walk around the outside of the hotel to where the party is being held in a large suite that has PRIVATE PARTY written on the board outside. There are loads of people there and, as we head toward the bar, they all want to stop and talk to Jon and congratulate him. He's all happy now, instead of showing the real uncertain side of himself like I saw in the car. That says something about his feelings for me if he can confide in me like that.

"Tilly, drink?" asks Bryan walking over to us. I nod. "Wine okay?" Another nod.

I'll be nodding in my sleep at this rate. He passes me a glass, and I take a large mouthful. Gross. I hate wine, especially red. I'd much rather have a beer. But I don't suppose that's Tilly's drink of choice. Come to think of it, I don't know if wine is either. From what I've seen, I think she's more of a hard liquor girl.

"Take it easy," says Jon leaning in and whispering in my ear. "I don't want you falling all over the place, especially as you're not used to drinking."

I am so. Except I can't tell him that, so I scowl at him instead, hoping he'll get the message.

"I'm not having a go," he adds. "But you hardly had anything to drink at the club the other week, and look how out of it you were." I shrug. He has a point, I suppose. "Come on, let's mingle. And remember, not a word." His arm rests in the small of my back, sending a shiver rippling through me, and he guides me toward a group of people.

True to his word, we spend the next hour *mingling,*

and my feet are killing me and my neck is aching from all the nodding. I tap Jon on the arm when there's a short lull in the latest conversation, and he leans in, putting his arm around my waist, which makes the hairs on the back of my neck stand up.

"I'm going to the bathroom," I whisper.

"Okay, I'll pop outside for a smoke." He kisses me on the cheek.

How come I didn't know he smoked? I hate smoking.

I follow Jon until we get to the entrance, and he takes a right toward the doors at the back, which lead out to the grounds.

"Don't be long," he calls over his shoulder as I go left.

I smile and nod.

There's nobody in the bathroom when I get there, so I decide to check out my Tilly smile and nod. Except I've hardly opened my mouth when I hear the door open, so I rush into one of the cubicles and sit down.

"Trust me," says a young-sounding girl with one of those high-pitched grating voices. "She's definitely on something."

"You don't know that," says the girl she's with.

"If she isn't, then tell me how come she looks so lifeless. Where's her usual sparkle? The fire? The reason she gets paid what she does."

I wonder who they're talking about. I didn't notice

anyone on drugs; then again, I'm not sure I know what to look for. If it's someone famous, Liv will love it. She loves celebrity gossip…if she ever talks to me again, of course. I mentally berate myself. Even to my ears, my thoughts are becoming repetitive. I should put all thoughts of Liv out of my mind instead of rehashing the *will she or won't she ever talk to me again* ones.

Except I can't stop feeling guilty about her, though I don't know why. It's not like I haven't tried to patch things up. And look at her, with Rich. She's probably leaving Matt all on his own now, which is nearly as bad as me missing her party because of Jon.

Sort of.

"Well, I love her," the nicer girl says.

"Whatever."

I don't like the sound of squeaky-voice girl. She seems nasty. What's the poor person they're talking about ever done to her? "I don't know what you've got against her. I love her movies." You go, girl.

"You know, she hooks up with all her producers."

"That's just gossip."

"Even if it is, you've got to admit she looks really rough tonight."

I figure they're talking about that woman, I can't think of her name, but she was in the comedy about a hairdresser. I noticed her earlier standing at the bar, and she didn't look that great. Her eyes and mouth had more lines around them than I remember her having on film, and her hair looked like it had been barely brushed. I wonder if it's true about her getting it on with all her producers. I bet Jon will know. I'll ask him later, once we get back to the hotel and I can actually open my mouth.

Then again, what if it's me they're talking about? But they said this person hooks up with her producers. I know Tilly has been with Dean and other guys, but no one has mentioned her with producers. I'm sure it's not her. I mean, me. Me as her. Whatever.

"Not her normal self, maybe. Not that I've ever seen her in the flesh before tonight."

"I met her once when I was filming in the L.A."

Ooohhhhh, that's interesting. Squeaky-voice girl must work in the movies. Though that's hardly surprising if she's at the party.

"Filming what? I didn't know you'd done any work over there."

"Well, I wasn't filming exactly. I'd gone with a friend for an audition, and we were at the same studio as she was."

"And you met her?"

"Kind of. Someone my friend knows was talking to her at a party, and we all stood together."

I hold my hand over my mouth to stifle a giggle. The one thing I've learned about this business is people are full of their own self-importance and like to exaggerate big time. I guess this girl qualifies on both counts.

"Does she still look the same?"

"No, that's what I was saying. There's no star quality about her tonight. I'm telling you, she's definitely on something, so I guess the rumors were right. Anyway, put your lipstick away and let's go. I really want an invite to the producer's party later."

"Will she be there?"

"I guess so, unless she's collapsed in a heap somewhere." Her voice gets fainter and I hear the door open. "I can imagine the headlines in the morning. Tilly Watson wasted again…"

The door closes.

Oh. My. God. It was me they were talking about all the time. I'm the one who looks like she's on drugs and out of it. This is so awful. What's Tilly going to think if I let her down tonight? Thing is, everyone on set says I look like her, so what have I done wrong? What should I do now? I can't go back inside, yet. I need to see Jon and tell him what happened so we can decide what to do together. He might want to go back to the hotel now, before I do any more damage. Hopefully he hasn't gone back inside already.

I smooth down my dress and take a quick look in the mirror to make sure I haven't smudged my makeup. I weigh the decision over whether to wear the sunglasses or not, and then I put them in my clutch. Tilly and I have similar round brown eyes, and maybe wearing the things indoors was part of what made me look like I'm high as a kite. I open the bathroom door and make my way to the rear entrance. Someone is looking out for me, because I don't bump into anyone on my way. When I get to the outside door, I push it open and look left and right. I can't see anyone, it's too dark, but I can hear voices coming from down the stone steps and off toward the left. I hold onto an iron banister and walk down. When I reach the bottom, my nostrils are assaulted by the disgusting smell of smoke. I want to turn back except the voices are now much clearer so I stay and listen.

"So, how do you think she's doing? It's uncanny how like Tilly she is." I recognize Bryan's voice.

He's talking about me. At least he thinks I'm doing okay. Maybe it's not as bad as I think it is. I wait, anxious, for the response.

"I know. I didn't think she'd be able to step up to the mark so well."

A shiver of excitement runs down my spine. It's Jon, and he's talking about me to Bryan. The girls in the bathroom were just being catty. I knew Jon wouldn't let me make a fool of myself.

"I didn't either," says Bryan. "And she's so easy to be with, not at all demanding, like Tilly. It's been a real pleasure working with her."

I wrap my arms around me and lean against the stair rail, smiling to myself. Heat radiates through my chest, and I feel so happy and content.

"Yes, she certainly takes direction well and never

utters a word when Zac starts hollering," says Jon.

Liv will never believe this when I tell her. Me being talked up by celebrities.

"And she's so easy to manipulate," Bryan says.

His words land like a ball of lead in my stomach. Manipulate? What does he mean by that?

"Yeah, I guess," Jon says.

See, Jon doesn't get what he means either. So screw you, Bryan.

"Of course, it helps that she's got the hots for you." Bryan laughs, a lot louder this time.

"Yes, it definitely helps."

"So what are you going to do about it? Would you date her?"

Beads of perspiration form on my brow. I don't care what they said about being able to manipulate me. It's Jon's answer to this question that's most important. Please let him say yes. Please.

"Nah. She's a sweet kid. But not my type. I've never gone for the sweet and innocent." He pauses.

But I can be different. I don't have to be *sweet and innocent*. I can be more like Tilly if he would just give me a chance. I ignore the voice in my head that's recoiling at my wanting to change for a boy.

"She did me a huge favor, though, coming here," he continues. "Getting 'Tilly' to this premiere was guaranteed publicity for the movie."

"Let her down gently, then. We might need her to

stand in for Tilly again."

"As long as she doesn't open her mouth." Jon says. "With her st-st-stutter, Hicksville accent, and ragdoll personality, it would be a disaster."

CHAPTER TWENTY

My body tenses, and it's all I can do to stop my legs from giving way. I want the earth to open up and swallow me whole. To take me somewhere safe. I'd give anything to discover that Jon hadn't really said what I just heard. That I ate or drank something that's giving me hallucinations. Anything. Except I know that's not true. I know that I'm here, and Jon's there with Bryan, and they're talking about me. ME.

My pulse is speeding, and my jaw's set so hard my teeth are aching. I've got to get away from here before anyone sees me. Especially Jon.

Somehow, I manage to force my legs into action, turn and half run, half stumble back up the steps, and all the time Jon's words are echoing over and over in my head. *Sweet. Innocent. Hicksville. Ragdoll. Sweet. Innocent. Hicksville. Ragdoll.*

And then Matt's words ring in my head. "They're so fake. Especially that Jon."

I've been such an idiot.

Reaching the top of the steps, I push open the door and then stop. Where should I go? No way am I going back into the party. How could I possibly face everyone knowing what they all think of me?

So where then?

I force myself to focus, except my mind's a total blank, until I suddenly remember the bathroom. I can go back there and be out of the way. And then think about what to do next.

Like I want to think.

Like I want to do anything other than crawl into a hole in the ground and stay there forever.

When I get to the bathroom, I go back into the stall I just vacated, sit down, place my head in my hands, and let out a long groan. I feel sick to my stomach. Never in my whole life has anyone been so awful to me.

Never. Never. NEVER.

All this time I thought Jon felt something for me, and that couldn't have been further from the truth. He only ever thought of me as sweet. *Sweet.* Who wants to be sweet? Or easy to manipulate? He was just using me. Even if it would be a *disaster* to have me open my mouth with my *stutter* and *Hicksville accent*. And I fell for it. God, I'm such an idiot. Liv and Matt were both right about him, but I chose to ignore all the signs.

Plus, it didn't just affect me. Look at all the times I have let my friends down. Not returning calls or texts. Not going to the dojo. Missing the party. Choosing the movie crowd over them. How would I feel if Liv and Matt gave me the brush off so often? I'd have been devastated. But they're better friends to me than I am to them, because they've never done anything like that to me. Okay, so maybe they've taken me for granted a bit in the past. But that's what being a friend is all about. It's definitely not about how I've been toward them.

And I've lied to Mom and Dad about who I'm here with, because I knew what they'd say if they found out the truth. I've been the biggest jerk on the planet. In the universe, even.

A low moan escapes my lips, and then the floodgates open. Tears pour down my cheeks, and I'm helpless to stop them. I rub my eyes with the back of my hand, and black smudges appear all over them. Running mascara. The least of my problems.

Why did I ever think Tilly's lifestyle was one to wish for? Even after seeing firsthand how it affects her. How it's destroying her. How she's hounded by the media, trashed by the public, and dumped on by her mom. Yet, I still wanted to be her. Wanted her *awesome* life. Wanted Jon.

Oh, God.

How stupid was I, thinking I'd have a chance with Jon? All those times when he put his arm around me and kissed me. Well, not *kissed* me, as in full-on, apart from the time he thought I was Tilly, but on the cheek. It was just a game to him. One big ego-boosting game. He knew I liked him, and he used it to his advantage. He probably went back and told Tilly how stupid I was being over him. Yeah. What fun they would've had at my expense. Their very own floor show.

Crap, crap, and a million, trillion times crap.

"Tilly, are you in there?" The sound of Jon's voice cuts into my thoughts.

He's outside. What should I do?

I can't face him. I just can't. Apart from the fact that my face must look disgusting with makeup smeared all over it, what would I say to him?

"I'm coming in."

NO. This is like…

I hear the door open and quickly jump on the seat so he can't see my feet if he looks under the door. I keep absolutely still for what seems like forever, praying he doesn't climb up and look over.

"She's not in here, Bryan," he says a few moments later, the frustration showing in his voice. "Where the hell's she gone now? She can't just disappear when we…" His voice fades away as the door closes behind him.

I can't believe what's happened. I'm so embarrassed about everything. And I never want to see Jon again.

Well, I'm not hanging around here, I'm going back to the hotel and then home. I come out of the stall and double check to make sure Jon really isn't here. I wouldn't put it past him to have pretended to have left to get me to come out.

He isn't here. No one is. Hopefully he's just gone back to the party and forgotten all about me. Though I guess that is hardly likely, knowing my luck. I check my face in the mirror and wipe away some of the black smudges with the back of my hand, but it doesn't make much difference. I don't care though, because all I'm going to do is go outside and flag down a cab to take me back to the hotel. Thank goodness I decided to bring some cash with me. I don't know why I did, because Jon had said I wouldn't need any.

I leave the bathroom and walk toward the entrance, keeping my head down. As I get to the door, I reach out and take hold of the big brass S-shaped handle.

"Abi. Tilly. Wait." I stop in my tracks and swallow hard, as my stomach plummets to the floor. So much for managing to avoid Jon.

"What are you doing?" Jon says, from behind me. "Everyone is wondering where you are. Quick, get…" I turn my head. "What the hell have you done to your face? You're spoiling everything, you silly girl."

Silly girl? How dare he? Suddenly, I'm fueled with such anger, it's like it's going to burst out of my whole body. "Me?" I shout. "Me spoiling everything? What about you?" I glare at him.

"What are you doing? Shut up, people will hear you." He grabs hold of my arm and squeezes it.

"I-I-I don't care if the whole world hears me!" I yank my arm away from him and rub it. "I've had it with you and all this." I sweep my arm back to indicate the gaudy lobby.

"Abi, please." His tone is softer, but I know it's fake. He's only trying to persuade me to do what he wants.

"Lay off the charm, Jon." Is that my voice? I've never sounded so sarcastic and in control before in my life. I must have learned more from Tilly than I realized.

"But…"

"Forget the *buts*. I know what you think of me."

"What are you talking about? You mean the world to me. Tell me why you're being like this. Come on, we've still got time to get you cleaned up and back in-side." He rests his arm across my shoulder, and I pull away.

"I'm not going back there. Not now. Not ever. *Sweet ragdoll Abi* won't be *manipulated* anymore."

It's like watching a slow-motion picture as my words penetrate. He goes from having a look of concern on his face, to a blank look, to one of shock. All in the space of a few seconds.

"You heard," he states quietly.

"Yes."

"We didn't mean anything by it."

"Yeah, right. And if you didn't mean it, I'm actually Tilly Watson. Look." I grab hold of my wig, pull it off, and wave it about furiously. "Now, if you'll excuse me, I'm going, and don't try to stop me." I take a step toward the door but stop when Jon's hand rests on my arm.

"Abi, please. We need you."

"Yes, to boost your reputation. Because it makes you seem special if you have Tilly on your arm. Or me pretending to be her, as long as I don't open my mouth, of course. And why should I care about that?" I fold my arms and assume Liv's I-am-a-wall-and-you're-not-getting-anything-past-me goalie stance. And it feels good.

"I'm sorry. You're right. I need you. You've no idea what I stand to lose if I screw this up."

Foolishly, I allow my eyes to lock with his, and my heart lurches. It must be hard for him, always living in Tilly's shadow. Really, she manipulates him as much as he's manipulated me. "Well…" I hesitate.

"I knew you'd understand. I'm relying on Tilly to pull a few strings and get me a part in her next movie. I can't jeopardize that now. Come on, let's fix you back up." His too-slick tone jolts me out of my Jon-induced trance. He has a self-satisfied smirk on his face, and it takes all my resolve not to smack it off. He's manipulating me again. I don't believe it. And to think I nearly fell for it.

Before I have time to reply, I'm blinded by a flash.

Jon swings round to face a man with a camera. "Stop now. Or you'll get more than a photo."

"Really?" The guy takes another shot. "Hey, Tilly... or whoever you are...look this way."

Jon lunges at him and tries to grab the camera, but the paparazzo steps to the side. Jon moves again, making a fist and drawing back his arm. But he's not quick enough. The guy gets out of the way, and Jon is left swinging his arm in mid-air.

Without thinking further, I lunge forward until I'm standing between them, easily deflecting Jon's ridiculous attempt at punching the other guy.

"Stop it," I snap, glaring from one to the other.

Don't ask me why, but they actually listen to me, and both remain glued to the spot. Probably shock more than anything. It's not every day someone my size tries to tackle two guys.

"You don't understand," Jon pleads with me. "If this goes viral, Tilly will be finished."

And he expects me to believe that's all he cares about? Hmmm? This is more to do with how he's going to look. Which, from where I'm standing, isn't good. Anyway, after all the other things Tilly's done, surely this will just be something else for her huge PR team to handle. I can't see it making any difference from her perspective.

"And I'm supposed to care? After what you did to me?" I say. "I hope *you're* finished. Tilly doesn't have it easy, and she deserves better than you."

"You tell him," the paparazzo says. "You know, doll, I don't know what's going on here, but TMZ would pay good money for your story."

"And you can shut up, too. You're no better than Jon," I reply glaring at him. "Tell TMZ they can cram it."

I turn to leave, and Jon makes a grab for me. But as soon as his hand touches my arm, I step to the side, transfer my weight onto my back leg, lift the other, and roundhouse-kick him in the chest. He loses his balance and his grip, and falls to the floor, and the paparazzo doesn't waste a second snapping shot after shot.

"That's how you take your opponent out," I say, looking down at his face and wondering what on earth I ever saw in him. "And it's also the last kickboxing lesson you'll ever get from me."

He opens his mouth to speak, but before he can even get the words out, I turn on my heels, go outside, and flag down a cab. All I want to do is go home.

CHAPTER TWENTY-ONE

I run through the hotel reception and through the double doors to the stairs, hoping that no one catches sight of me. When I get to my level, I race along the corridor and then use my keycard to open the door to my hotel room. Then I slam the door behind me and lean against it. I'm screwed. There's no way I can go back home on the private plane, I'll have to get there another way.

How can everything be so good one minute and the next minute it all comes crashing down around me? It's just not fair.

I don't know what to do.

I don't know how I feel.

I don't know anything, apart from the fact that I want Liv.

She'll tell me what to do. And she won't judge either. Even if she does think to herself that it's my fault. Which I wouldn't blame her for thinking.

Except, how can it be all my fault? I tried so hard to do everything right. Surely I can't be to blame foreverything? Then again, maybe I'm deluding myself by thinking that I've been totally blameless in all this.

I have to talk to her. But, of course, I'll never get her to take my call. So what's the point? Well, if I can't speak to her, I'll phone Mom instead. At least she'll talk to me, even if she won't like what I'll be telling her.

I pull out my cell from my purse, but before I call, something inside tells me to stop.

What am I doing?

Rhetorical question. I know what I'm doing. What I always do. Looking to someone else to sort out my problem. All my life I've turned to Mom and Dad, or Liv, or Matt. Well, not any more. It's about time I took control myself. Okay, having a stutter hasn't exactly made my life easy (even if I am able to control it most of the time), but I'm an adult, and from now on *I'm* going to be in charge of me.

Just the thought of it sends my heart racing and the adrenaline flowing, but not in a bad way. I sort of feel empowered.

I sit on the couch to think through my options.

With a clear head, I now realize that getting home isn't going to be a problem. All I need to do is go online and book a flight. Simple. So, I reach for my cell and then take out my credit card, find a flight, and reserve a seat. The only problem is the flight takes off in under two hours, so I have to leave right away.

While getting my things together, I catch a glimpse of myself in the bedroom mirror and realize I'm still in makeup, including the nose. All I have time to do is wipe the black mascara stains from my face and brush my hair. At least without the wig I look a lot less like Tilly.

I take the elevator to the ground and walk through the hotel with no one staring at me. Thank goodness.

"Want a cab, miss?" the doorman asks as I leave the hotel.

"Yes, please. To the airport," I reply.

In an instant, there's a cab pulling up alongside me, and I flash him a grateful smile.

The ride takes about forty minutes, during which time I stare out the window and watch the lights of New York. Even at this time of night, there are still loads of people around. It's so different from Omaha. I'd love to come back and explore one day.

It sort of feels like I'm in a movie; nothing's quite real. There are bound to be some repercussions from the studio. Damaging their reputation or something. But it's not all my fault. If Tilly hadn't got wasted, then none of this would have happened, so really she should take some of the blame.

"We're here," says the driver, over his shoulder.

"Thanks." I didn't even notice we'd stopped driving.

After giving him the last of my dollars, I head toward the door for departures and then walk up to the check-in desk and wait in line for my boarding pass. It doesn't take long and, glancing at my watch, I see that there's about thirty minutes before we board. I manage to find an empty seat near the TV, except the only thing on is the news. Which is boring. In fact, I'm just about to get up and go to the bathroom when someone familiar on the screen catches my eye.

It's me.

Me as Tilly, taking off my wig.

• • •

It's now four-thirty in the morning. Scanning the people waiting as we come through arrivals, my heart's in my mouth. I texted Matt just before take-off asking him to meet me at the airport, but he didn't reply. I didn't know who else to ask. I'm just hoping that he'll forget how I've been, at least for the moment, and be here.

"Abi." I hear my name and see Matt waving, a grim expression on his face.

It's not rocket science to work out that he'd rather be anywhere else than here waiting for me. But at least he's still here, as he's always been when I've needed him. Tears form in my eyes, but I fight them back while heading over to him. "Thanks for coming," I say, not making eye contact in case they start again.

He shrugs and then walks away, his hand jammed into his pockets. He leaves me to follow. I've ruined everything between us.

When we reach his car I put my bag into the trunk and then get in next to him. "Thanks," I say again.

"I'd hardly leave you alone in the middle of the night, would I?"

Of course not. Because he's a true friend. Or he was once.

"I guess not."

I focus on my knees, wishing I could turn back the clock to before Bill mentioned this whole stunt double thing. Those so-called feelings I had for Jon were just crap. They weren't real. I got sucked into the glitz and glamour of everything. And ended up losing the best thing I ever had. Matt. Okay, I know that he didn't feel the same as me. But I had his friendship. Now I don't even have that.

"And what on earth made you travel looking like that?"

I glance at Matt and see the disdain on his face. Then I pull down the visor and look in the mirror at Tilly's nose. Tilly's makeup. And my hair.

Who the hell am I?

Chapter Twenty-two

I creep into the house, trying not to make a noise in case it wakes Mom and Dad, except I trip and stumble into the hall table, and the books and keys on top fall to the floor with a crash.

"Who's there?" Dad yells from the top of the stairs.

Which isn't a good idea if it really was an intruder. Maybe I'll mention that to him later.

"Dad, it's me," I call.

"Abi?"

"Abi?" Mom repeats. "What are *you* doing home? Is everything okay?"

Before I have time to answer, she's hurrying down the stairs, with Dad close behind.

"Not really. It was awful, he…" My voice breaks.

"Sweetheart, what's wrong? Are you hurt?" She runs down the last few stairs and engulfs me in a hug. My body goes limp, and a groan escapes my lips.

"What's happened?" Dad asks. "Has someone done something to you? I'll kill them!"

"No." I sniff, pulling out of Mom's hold. "No one's hurt me."

"Well, something must have happened to make you like this," Mom says. "Why have you come home in the middle of the night instead of tomorrow, like you said you would?"

"Because I found out the truth about what they're really like. They were just using me. I thought that Jon was my friend…"

"Jon, as in Tilly's boyfriend?" Her voice increases in volume.

"Yes. I was with him tonight."

"What about Tilly?"

"Tilly couldn't go to the premiere, so they asked me to go as her instead. In full makeup. To protect her reputation, they said. And I said yes. I thought it would be fun and exciting."

"Why would it protect her reputation?" Mom asks.

"They thought if she didn't go, the media would say it was because she was out of her head somewhere. It made sense to me because you know what the press is like. In this instance, they'd have been right. She couldn't go, because she got wasted the night before."

"So, what happened last night to change every-thing?" Mom asks.

Everything.

"I found out some of the people who were supposed to be my friends were just using me. Jon didn't want to protect Tilly's reputation. He was just looking out for himself. He wanted to be seen with Tilly on his arm." I swallow hard. "I've made a total idiot of myself. They don't care about me, not really. They never did."

Saying it aloud is really painful.

Mom puts her arm around me again. "Try not to think about it. I know it hurts, but you don't need them. You've got some great friends who love you for being you."

"*Had*, you mean. I've ruined everything. Liv hates me because I let her down over her party. And Matt… well, if it wasn't for the kickboxing, he wouldn't want to know me either."

"Liv doesn't hate you. Talk to her. You'll sort it out, I'm sure."

"Let's leave it 'til the morning," Dad says. "The main thing is you're not hurt."

Well, maybe not physically. Mentally, it's another matter.

"Good idea," Mom says. "Let's wipe your eyes and go to bed, and we'll talk more tomorrow." She passes me a tissue from the box on the side and then walks me toward the stairs. My body starts to relax, closely followed by the hugest guilty feeling ever flooding through me.

I can't believe what I've done. I'll make it up to everyone. I really will. To Liv, Matt. Mom and Dad. To everyone.

. . .

I stretch out, and glance over at the clock beside my bed. It's two-thirty. What am I doing in bed at this time?

Oh, crap.

I remember.

All of it.

After a long, hot shower, I pull on my jeans and tee shirt and go downstairs to the kitchen, where I can hear the TV blaring. Mom's a total TV addict, keeps it on all day. She says it's for the background noise it makes. She hates it when it's too quiet.

Judging by the smell, Mom's doing her usual weekend baking. Man, I could kill for one of her chocolate muffins.

"Hungry?" Mom asks as I walk through the door.

She must have read my mind.

"You could say that."

She puts a muffin on a plate and passes it to me, then flicks the switch on the kettle. "With a hot chocolate, too?"

"Yes, please."

"How are you feeling?" Dad asks as he comes into the kitchen. He walks past and ruffles my hair.

"Dad, don't," I say in a sort of sharp tone, but I don't really mean it. It feels good to be back to normal.

Mom gives me my drink and pulls out a couple of kitchen chairs. We both sit down, and Dad leans against the worktop facing us.

I wrap my hands around my mug of chocolate. The smell and the warmth are so relaxing.

Suddenly, the volume on the TV gets louder, and I notice Dad pointing the remote at it. "Turn it down, not up," Mom says, glancing away from me.

"It's that girl," says Dad. "She's got that look on her face. You know, the one you have, Abi, when you've done something wrong and you're not sure of the repercussions."

I sit back in my chair, and we all face the TV. It's Tilly sitting behind a table, with her *mom*. Since when do I look like that?

"She's giving a press conference," says Mom, sounding all knowledgeable.

"Who's that?" asks Dad, looking at the photo on the screen of me from last night.

"It's me, Dad. My argument with Jon, when I pulled off my wig, got caught by one of the paparazzi and…"

"Quiet," says Mom. "Tilly's speaking."

I glance back up at the TV. Tilly looks all contrite. But she knew what we were doing, so surely she's not going to try and get out of it?

"I've been under a lot of stress recently and came down with the flu after a difficult shooting schedule," Tilly says, her voice weak and pathetic.

"Flu? That's debatable," I say.

"Sssshhh," say Mom and Dad, together.

"Sorrryyyy." Okay, that may sound belligerent, but really…

"My manager persuaded my stand-in on the movie to go to the premiere as me. Unfortunately, I was so sick, I didn't really register what I'd agreed to."

"Jon said she knew and was all for it…" I pause for a moment. "But I guess that's just another lie he told me," I say, realizing that Tilly has probably been used as much as me. And not just by Jon. I wasn't much better, wanting to steal him from her, however much I denied it to Liv. And to myself, to be honest.

"Who was the stand-in?" calls out one of the journalists.

I hold my breath. Please don't let her say my name. *Please*. It would be the most awful thing in the world if everyone found out it was me.

"I'm not prepared to say," says Tilly, lowering her eyes. "I don't blame her at all for what happened. She was manipulated. Just like me."

Thank you, Tilly. Whatever your reason for not naming me. "And your manager?" calls another journalist.

"He's history," says Tilly's mom, leaning in front of

her daughter to speak into the mic. She looks nothing like Tilly. Her hair is short and so blond it's almost white. She has a hardness about her that creeps me out. "He took advantage of my little girl while she was sick. No more questions. Tilly needs to rest." She puts her arm around Tilly's shoulders, and Tilly visibly relaxes into her.

Tilly's either doing a first-rate acting job, or she's sorted out some of the problems she has with her mom. I know I'd just die if she was my mom, but whatever she's like, she's Tilly's. However old I am, I couldn't bear not to have Mom there, looking out for me. The thought sends a shiver down my spine.

"Ridiculous," Dad says, cutting into my thoughts. He presses the remote and turns off the TV. "Forget it, Abi. The whole thing will be a five-minute wonder. Mark my words."

"What do you mean?" I ask.

"By tomorrow they'll be looking for the next story, and you'll be old news."

I hope he's right, I really do.

"He's right," Mom says. "So try not to worry."

The front door bell goes before I have time to answer. "I'll go," I say walking out of the kitchen.

I open the door, and my stomach plummets to the floor and back again. Holy crap.

"Tilly?" I can't believe she's standing at the door smiling at me. "But I was just watching you on TV. How did you get from there to here so quickly?"

"Magic," she says, laughing. "We recorded it an hour ago. May I come in? I don't want to stay outside in case I'm recognized."

I scan the street, and all I can see is a cab at the bottom of our drive, which is probably waiting for Tilly. There doesn't seem to be anyone spying on us. But you never know with the paparazzi; they can be hiding in the most ridiculous places.

"Yes. Of course. Sorry. I'm just in shock seeing you here."

And not just that. Seeing her here smiling and being friendly. It's got to be the most surreal experience of my life.

I step to the side and wait for her to come inside and then close the door behind her.

"Thanks," she says.

We stare at each other for a few seconds, not speaking. I'm so ashamed of what I've done. To everyone, including Tilly.

"I'm so sorry about what happened. I got so caught up in Jon's charm. I didn't stop to think about what that meant for you," I say the words falling out of my mouth at ninety miles an hour. "And…"

"It doesn't matter," Tilly says, interrupting me. She rests her hand on my arm. "Jon's a jerk. He uses people. He used you. He used me. Well, he tried to use me. But I got him back." A smug expression crosses her face. I don't think I want to know what she's done. Although, I won't be too upset if he pays a little for what he did.

"Well, I'm still sorry. Thanks for not telling the press my name. I behaved like such an idiot, especially to my friends. I can never forgive myself for that." I lean against the wall my arms folded across my chest.

"Thanks for sticking up for me with Jon. Especially since I haven't always been that nice to you. No one's ever done that before." Tilly's voice is tentative. She's not as sure of herself as she makes it look. Maybe we're more similar that I first thought. But more to the point how does she know what I said to Jon?

"You heard? How?"

"You went viral. Someone filmed it on their phone, I guess. Check it out, and see Jon's face when you told him I deserved someone better." Tilly does an impression of Jon with his eyes and mouth wide open. So funny.

"I meant it."

"Thanks. You know, I'd like to think that we could be friends."

I repeat. This is so surreal.

"Sure. Yes. I'd like that."

Liv will be beside herself with excitement when she finds out.

"I'm sorry for all the times I've mocked your stutter. That was really mean of me."

"Don't worry about it. I've had a lot worse over the years." I shrug, like it's not important. In a way it isn't.

The main thing is we've moved past it.

"That's still no excuse," Tilly says. She gets a faraway look in her eyes. "Every time I've let down my guard, someone sold me out to the media for money. When you turned down the TMZ offer, I couldn't believe it. You're the first person I've ever seen actually do that." Then she snaps out of it and focuses hard on my face. "You know, you haven't stuttered once since I've been here."

She's right. I hadn't even thought about it until this moment.

"I usually don't stutter when I'm with friends."

"Really?" She smiles, and it reaches up to her eyes and lights up her face. It feels like this is the first time I've seen the genuine Tilly.

"Really." I say, beaming back her. "You still haven't said why you're here."

I'm finding it hard to get my mind around this new and improved Tilly. Not that I'm complaining.

"To meet your mom. And to sample her chocolate muffins. That's okay, isn't it?"

Without further thought, I fling my arms around her and give her a hug. It's funny how we are exactly the same height and build. I know everyone had always said that, but I didn't get it until now.

"Yes. She'd love that."

We head for the kitchen. "Mom, I've got someone I want you to meet," I call out.

Chapter Twenty-three

"I bet you really hate me, don't you?" I ask Liv, after explaining everything to her, hardly daring to look her in the eye.

As soon as Tilly left, I came right over to see Liv. It surprised me that she let me into her house. I thought she'd tell me to go away, but she didn't. She was prepared to hear me out, even if she wasn't her usual warm self with me. But I didn't mind.

"What I don't get is that you were happy to hook up with this Jon. Someone else's boyfriend. That's not you," Liv replies, shaking her head.

"I know," I say, waving my arms in frustration. "It was like everything I believed in just went out the window. I acted like a jerk, and I'm so sorry. If I could have your party night over again, I wouldn't let you down. It was just I was with Jon, and I thought he really liked me, and it got later and later, and I got more and more wasted. Anyway, that's just an excuse, and I don't want to give you excuses for being a crap friend. The joke's on me though. He was just using me. Serves me right for trying to take him from Tilly. God, how stupid does that sound, like I could ever do anything like that? I'm such a freakin' idiot."

Liv comes over to where I'm standing in her kitchen and gives me a hug. "No you're not. Jon is, for treating you like that. And Tilly."

"I really thought we had something going, but we didn't. There wasn't anything between us. He knew about my feelings for him, and he played with them to make me do what he wanted."

"It didn't work, though. Did it? Not in the end." She giggles.

"You should have seen his face when I pulled off the wig. That paparazzo got some great shots of it." I start to laugh. I'm not sure whether it's because I'm finding everything funny, or from relief that Liv still wants to be friends. But I don't care. It feels good, whatever the reason. It hits me that with everything going on, I haven't laughed like this in a long time.

"I wish I had," she says. "Now you and Tilly are friends, too. And that's sick."

"Yes, we are. I'm glad. Though I doubt we'll see

much of each other, since we don't exactly frequent the same social circles." I can't help giggling to myself at the thought of Tilly hanging out with us at Chelsea's. Or wandering around the mall doing nothing much.

"It's still awesome to have someone like her as a friend. Maybe you can introduce us."

"Sure. She'll be in town in a few weeks, and we've arranged to meet. She's flying up here for another audition."

Let's just hope that she keeps herself clean, like she promised. Then she'll be able to get her career back on track. And she knows she can come and see us anytime. Mom really liked her. If anyone can help get Tilly back on the straight and narrow, it's Mom.

"That would be so cool." Her eyes are bright with anticipation. "Now tell me, what was it like at the premiere? Did you see loads of celebs?"

Typical of Liv to ask about that, after all I've been through. But I don't mind, I'm happy to answer every single one of her questions. Because hopefully it means she's forgiven me.

"At the party I saw quite a few. There was the girl from *The Hunger Games*. She looked amazing, and she was with that guy from *Bones*." I chew on my bottom lip trying to remember who else was there.

"Girl. Guy. Come on Abi, give me names." She places her hands on her hips and tries to look fierce. Except she spoils it by smirking.

"You know me. I don't know who they all are. I'm trying to remember, really I am."

"See, I always said you were wasted on the movie business." She shakes her head. "Hey, want to go into town? We could go to Starbucks."

"I don't know. I ought to go home and be with Mom and Dad after everything I've put them through."

"They won't mind. Call them. I bet they're just glad to have the old Abi back."

"Yeah, right. The plain old Abi."

"That's the one. Say yes. Go on. We can invite Matt and Rich to come with us and we'll have a great time."

"YES," I shout, suddenly remembering. "Rich. I want to hear all about him. I can't believe you hooked up with him."

"He's so cool." A dreamy look washes over her face, and I burst out laughing.

"Oh my God. Look at you. I can't believe how bad you've got it. Do I really want to go out with the two of you? I bet you're all over each other, and I'll just be in the way."

I'm so happy for her.

"I've already said we can ask Matt, too."

"Except we're not like you and Rich. We're just friends. Not even friends if the last time we saw each other is anything to go by."

"I'm sure we can do something about that."

"What do you mean?" I ask, frowning.

"Come on Abi, you and Matt are a couple waiting to happen."

If she'd said that to me six months ago, how excited would I have been? I'd have even admitted how I felt to her, instead of trying not to think about it. But that was before I met Jon and realized that my feelings for Matt couldn't have been what I thought they were. Except now I'm not sure. Because my feelings for Jon definitely weren't what I thought *they* were. Which means I was probably right about my feelings for Matt all along. I just got sidetracked by Jon.

"You're talking absolute crap. Matt is my friend. *Was* my friend. He doesn't think much of me now, he could hardly bring himself to even look at me when took me home last night, let alone talk."

"That's because he's trying to protect himself from his feelings for you. Because he thinks you don't feel the same way. Ever since you got the movie gig, he's been jealous as hell and trying not to show it. But he can't fool me."

My jaw drops. She can't be serious. Matt has feelings for me? No way.

"That's crazy. Matt and I are just friends, and he's never given the slightest indication that he thinks of me in any other way."

I'd have noticed if he did, that's for sure.

"So, if he asked you out, you'd say no?"

"He won't ask me, so that's a pointless question."

"Yes, but if he did. Would you go?"

"I repeat, your question is pointless, especially when you think of what's just happened between us. I've screwed up royally with him. And our friendship is now hanging by a thread."

"Well, don't tell me that you haven't thought about it. Because I know you have." She wags her finger under my nose.

"How?" I exclaim. I can feel myself coloring now at the thought of being so obvious about my feelings. I really thought I had everything under wraps.

"It wasn't hard to work out. The way you stared at him when you thought no one was looking. The way you'd sometimes go red when he entered the room. And look how jealous you would get when he went out with all those other girls."

"I did not get jealous," I say emphatically.

Which is a total lie. I hated it when Matt saw other girls. Not that they were ever serious. But it didn't matter. I hated it anyway.

"Hmmm. This is me you're talking to."

She's right. I can't hide anything from her; she knows me too well.

"Liv, will you stop it? Matt isn't going to ask me out, even if I do want him to. I'll admit now that at one time I *did* want to. I used to imagine us going out together." I pause for a moment. "And, more to the point, if you knew this, then why didn't you say anything?"

She's my friend. We share everything. Almost. It makes no sense for her not to ask me about it.

"I don't know," a guilty expression crosses her face. "I guess I didn't want to change anything. I love it just being the three of us. I thought if I pushed the two of you together I'd be left out. Sorry."

"Don't say sorry. It's not your fault. I was the same about not wanting to change anything. I worried that Matt didn't feel the same, so if he somehow found out my feelings, then everything would end. Then I had this thing for Jon and thought that I'd gotten over Matt."

"And have you?"

"No. If anything, I think more of him. When I compare him to that idiot Jon, there is no comparison. But I'm afraid. He cuts and runs when things get too serious with one of his girlfriends."

She flashes me a knowing smile. "You have no idea, do you?"

I blink stupidly at her. "What?"

"Well, maybe you should ask him about that," Liv says, arching a brow.

Suddenly, it hits me. She's right. I have to find out myself if there's a chance for us.

"I will."

. . .

"And a cinnamon donut, please," I say to Liv as she

heads to the counter with Rich, leaving me sitting at the table alone with Matt.

Although the way my stomach's churning there's no way on earth that I'm going to take a single bite. I've done nothing since we arranged to meet the guys except think about what I'm going to say to Matt. And I still haven't decided.

Judging by the long line, we could be alone for quite a while, which means now is my chance. First of all, I want to sort out us being friends. Then, if he's okay with that, I think I'll take it one step further. At least, that's the plan. If I have the courage. If only he wasn't sitting there looking so distant.

I bite on my bottom lip. Looks like it's now or never. And I feel totally sick inside. What if he won't forgive me? I know Liv has, but it doesn't automatically mean that Matt will. It will kill me if he doesn't, if I've ruined our friendship forever.

"I'm sorry for everything that's happened recently."

"Whatever." He shrugs.

He's not making it easy for me. Then again, why should he? I don't deserve him to just roll over and act like everything is cool. Because I know it isn't.

"I shouldn't have put the movie crowd before you and Liv. If you don't want to be friends with me anymore, I understand."

Understand, yes. Forgive myself, no.

"Forget it," he drawls, a hint of a smile playing about

his lovely mouth. "I'm glad to have the real Abi back."

I swallow hard. I know I didn't say anything to Liv when she said the same thing, but I should have. Because this *real* Abi that they keep talking about isn't me anymore.

"You know, I'm not the same as I was before. Not counting the way I dropped you and Liv and what happened with Jon, the movie experience has been really good. I'm different now. I don't have to rely on you and Liv, or Mom and Dad to fight my battles for me. I can stand up for myself. Do things I wouldn't have done before."

It's funny that it took Liv and Matt talking about the *real* Abi for me to realize just how much I've changed. I have to say it feels good. Really good. So maybe I should thank Jon for what he did.

"Like that roundhouse kick of yours that went viral?" He smiles. "I know that. And I'm happy for you. It's cool you can do things for yourself now. But what I'm glad to have back is the Abi who isn't selfish and who supports her friends. Who's there for us. I'm sorry if in the past we tried to take over, but it was only because we love you."

The gravelly way he says "love you" makes my heart do a flip, which happens again when he gives me a long, lazy smile. Without thinking, I gaze into his green-and-gold eyes, then, realizing what I'm doing, shake myself out of it. There's still a part of me that doesn't want to reveal how I feel, how I've always felt, how I'm afraid of changing us for the worse.

"Don't apologize," I finally manage. "I let you and Liv decide what I do. I'm happy that we're talking again. I hated when we weren't."

"Me too," he says so sweetly that my feelings for him come crashing to the surface.

This is insane. I know I decided to tell him, but do I really want to risk everything? Then again, I can't stop thinking about what Liv said about him liking me as more than a friend. And when I tried to fool him into thinking I was Tilly, he could see right through the disguise. He said he'd always know me. That must mean something.

"So everything's good between us then?" I ask, trying to sound casual despite the thumping of my heart against my ribcage. "Because there's something I want to ask you."

"Sure." His eyes lock with mine.

A flush creeps up my cheeks, and there's nothing I can do to hide it.

"You know when you said you could recognize me, no matter how much crap I had on my face? What did you mean by that?"

He stares intently into my eyes. It's like the whole coffee shop falls away, and it's just the two of us floating in a hazy mist. "Exactly that. You can dress up and pretend to be someone else, but you'll never be able to hide who you are from me. Because you shine through everything. Forget the glitz and glamour. Just be yourself. No one can compete with that."

I try to catch my breath. That's the most eloquent I've ever heard him. And judging by the embarrassed expression on his face, he's not likely to repeat it.

"Thanks. That's the nicest thing anyone has ever said to me." And then I know that now is the right time to ask. "There's something else," I say, beads of sweat forming on my forehead.

"Yeah?"

"Um. W-w-we've been friends for a long time, haven't we?"

A line of worry forms between his eyes. "You never stutter with me. Not with me." He pauses a moment. "But yes," he replies, nodding.

"Best friends."

"Always." He nods again.

My heart is pounding in my ears, and I'm clenching and unclenching my fists in my lap. Who knew this would be so hard? Well, actually, I did. But I'm going to do it. If he says yes, then it will be like all of my birthdays coming at once. *But what if he says no?*

I'll live. I can't play it safe any longer.

"I didn't think you'd be interested in anything else, but Liv said…and I hoped…if she's right…and…whether you and I…whether you could…you know…"

"What?" he asks, his eyes twinkling.

He knows what I'm asking. He's going to say yes. I know it.

"Be my boyfriend," I blurt out. "Because I've loved you since I was eight."

For a moment, he goes still. Combat still. Why did I open my mouth? It's not like I don't know what Matt's like. My heart feels empty at the thought of what I've done to our friendship, and I want to run for the hills.

But then his face lights up in that big, boyish grin I know so well, one I haven't seen since I started being horrible to him during my short movie career. He leans forward and takes my hands from my lap and holds them in his. Then he kisses me gently on the lips.

It feels so right. So perfect. He tastes like cinnamon and coffee and all of my birthdays rolled into one.

"Matt?" I say finally, murmuring his name against his lips as I dimly realize that the entire coffee shop has burst into applause.

"Mmm?" He dives in for another kiss.

"Matt?"

Something in my voice makes him back away. "What is it?"

"The other girls. You always bolt when things get intense. Remember? You don't do meeting the parents. You don't do serious."

A corner of his mouth quirks upward. "You really don't know, do you?" he asks, echoing Liv's earlier words.

I'm completely at a loss. "Know what?"

"It wasn't that they were serious." The smile he gives me then is so vulnerable, it's devastating. "It's that they weren't you, Abi."

I'm so full of emotion, I don't have any words to respond. So I pull him toward me for another kiss, not even caring that I'm treating the coffee shop full of people to another show. Somewhere in the background, I hear Liv cheering.

And to think I wanted to be like Tilly. Not freakin' likely. I have all I want here.

Finally, I feel like the real Abi Saunders has arrived.

And for exclusive sneak peeks at our upcoming books, excerpts, contests, chats with our authors and editors, and more…

Be sure to like us on Facebook

Follow us on Twitter @entangledteen

And follow us on Instagram @entangledteen

Acknowledgments

Once again, this book would not exist without the help of my fabulous critique partners, Amanda Ashby and Christina Phillips.

To everyone at Entangled Publishing, thank you for publishing my book. I particularly want to thank Tracy Montoya and Shannon Godwin for your incredibly insightful edits. I'd also like to mention Debbie Suzuki; thanks for your hard work in promoting my book. Thanks, also, to Kelley York for yet another amazing cover.

Finally, to my husband, Garry, and children, Alicia and Marcus, thanks for all your support and understanding.

Chapter One

Early June
Now

One, two, three, four. I focus to slow my breathing. In, out, in, out, trying to make the breaths stretch slowly, closer to tortoise rather than hare, like they're rushing right now. My palms sweat, making my hands stick to the steering wheel, almost like they're in clay on my pottery wheel.

Why am I so nervous? I shouldn't be. This is Jason and he loves me. How many times has he assured me I can tell him anything? That we're connected...soul mates, who were lucky enough to find each other in this crazy, screwed-up world we live in.

More than that, he likes it when I talk to him, when I tell him what's inside me. Because at home, all he has is ugliness. Fighting parents, a dad who is always putting him down and calling him names.

I'm his haven. His beautiful.

Funny how out of all the billions of people in the whole wide world, I found him. That he calls me his beautiful when that's what Dad always called Mom. Not in the same words—la mia bella signora is what Dad used to call her. My beautiful lady. That's how I knew Jason and I were meant to be. It was a sign that I'm destined for a love just as true as my parents had. Just like I always felt it was destiny for them to adopt me. She was meant to be my mom.

My heart starts to calm at the memory of Jason whispering those words to me. Of his breath against my ear. His body wrapped around mine. *We love each other,* I remind myself, so I shouldn't be scared to tell Jason. Now the rest of it? That makes my stomach turn and my head pound. Dad is going to freak.

After pulling the keys from the ignition, I get out of my car, running my hands down my red dress. It's the one I wore the night we met.

If red wasn't my favorite color before, it definitely is now. He'd touched my hair, the red that surprises everyone, since Dad is Italian. But then, it's not as though I would look like him.

That quickly, it had been like Jason and I knew each other forever. Did he know then? Feel the draw he told me about later? Feel the same spark with me that Mom always talked about with Dad? I hadn't at first. I didn't want to feel anything when I met Jason. Caring hurt, and I had enough hurt to last a lifetime.

I love him now, though. That's what matters.

Red hair…red dress, and now red cheeks. I never knew blushing could be so damn sexy…

Half of me wanted to laugh at him. I mean, really? How dumb did he think I was? At the time, it was obvious his words were lines, but instead of laughing, I talked to him. He talked back, and nothing's been the same ever since.

Smiling, I start to walk toward his brother Sam's house. Luckily, he's always out of town, so we never have to worry about seeing him. It's the perfect place for Jason and me to meet.

The front door swings open before I get a chance to knock. Jason's there, his blond hair messy like always. He's wearing a pair of shorts, no shirt. Even after the past three months, I still shiver seeing his toned body. The ripples of his abs and firm arms. He works out like crazy.

"Hey, babe. About time you got here. Sam will be home soon, so we don't have much time to hang out."

As soon as he pulls me inside, his mouth is on mine. So recognizable, that mint tinged with smoke. I've always hated smoking, which is why he sucks on the mints. But still, the mixture is him. I would know it anywhere. It's not that I necessarily like it, but it's familiar. And familiarity is important.

Tell him, tell him, tell him. The words creep into my head.

I try to slam the door on them, but they're like his smoke, floating under the door and filling the room until I'm almost suffocating on them. "Jason…" I pull back a little bit. "I want to talk to you, remember? I have… I have something to tell you."

He smiles, threading his fingers through mine before pulling me farther into the house. Into the living room. "Sorry, I just missed you. You know how irresistible you are to me."

I feel the heat burning my cheeks.

"Ah, there is it. Love that blush."

Somehow, it's those words that give me the courage I need. He loves my blush, my laugh. How many times has he told me he loves everything about me?

Love will make it okay.

"I…" I grab his other hand, too, needing to touch him as much as I can, wanting to look him in the eyes when I speak to him. "I need to tell you something important."

He cocks his head a little, his hands tightening. "What is it?"

"I'm…" *Push the words out, Brynn.* They've been eating me alive for weeks and now I just need to *say* them. My hands start shaking and briefly I wonder if he can feel it. My throat feels clogged, like words or breath can't get through. They're trapped behind a barrier of fear. *Do it!* "I'm pregnant."

The sentence somehow sucks all the air out of the room. It's suddenly hard to breathe again. Jason's hands grip mine tighter and tighter. I steady myself, proud of how I'm handling this. I spent two days crying before today, freaking out. I promised myself I wouldn't freak when I told Jason.

"Excuse me?"

"I'm pregnant...with a baby. Duh, of course it's a baby, but your baby...*our* baby." I step closer to him, but he pulls away. His hands jerk out of my grasp.

"How the fuck are you pregnant, Brynn? It sure as hell can't be mine. I've worn a condom every time we've been together. Every. Single. Time." His words make me flinch. They're like a whip biting into my skin.

Tears blur my vision; anger tries to block them. I'm shocked that Jason could accuse me of something like this. Then I remember the stories he's told me, the anger he lives with every day. I promised Jason I wouldn't be like that. *We* wouldn't be that way.

But he made *me* the same promise, too.

Locking eyes on him, I notice his face is red, see the angry set of his jaw as he crosses his arms. Who is this? Jason has never yelled at me before. "I don't know... I don't know. But I'm pregnant. I swear. I've heard stories about girls getting pregnant even with a condom. Maybe it, like, had a hole in it. This isn't something I would lie about, Jason. I've never been with anyone but you. Only you. You know that."

My hands shake. My heart, too. I love him. *But he thinks I would cheat on him.* The anger tries to push its way in again, but I swallow it down until it creates this sort of vacuum inside me instead. Blood rushes through my ears, making it difficult to focus on anything else.

"Hate to break it to you, Brynn, but if you haven't been with anyone but me, you wouldn't be knocked up right now."

A chill sweeps over me. The air conditioner? Whatever it is, it feels strong enough to knock me over. No, break me apart, blowing pieces of me around the house. I shake my head, trying to make sense of what he's saying. Trying to swallow down the need to vomit. "How can you say that? You know I love you. I'd never. I love *you*, Jason."

He laughs. I used to love the sound, and now it's beating me into the ground, sounding so different from any of his laughs before. "Didn't you tell me your little boyfriend broke up with you the day before we got together? I'm sure you loved him, too. Grow up. I swear, you're so naive."

How many times have I told him I never loved Ian? The only other time I thought I was in love, I was a dumb kid… Kid…

This can't be happening. Jason can't be treating me this way. Not when I'm going to have our baby. A *baby*. I clutch my stomach. The word suddenly starts repeating over and over in my head, blurring and mixing with Jason's angry accusations until it's all I can hear or feel.

"Jesus, I'm such a fucking idiot!" He runs a hand through his hair. "How long have you known? Who told you? Figured you'd try and trap me, did you? Hate to break it to you, but it's not going to happen."

"What?" The word manages to tumble out of my mouth.

He's pacing now, and my eyes dart around the room, following him. It's a struggle when I can't stop his voice in my head or the nausea in my stomach.

Hate to break it to you, Brynn, but if you haven't been with anyone but me, you wouldn't be knocked up right now.

"This isn't a game, Brynn. This is my life. I could go to fucking jail over this shit. You have to get rid of it. I'll give you money or whatever, but you have to get rid of it."

Dizziness twists and turns around me, pulling me in, dragging me under. *Jail... Get rid of it...*

Oh, God. I'm pregnant. I'm sixteen and pregnant. He wants me to get rid of our baby. My dad will never talk to me again.

With Jason by my side, I thought it would be okay. Thought we could make it work. I'd have someone else to love.

My eyes flutter and my legs go weak. I crumple to the floor, not sure what else to do. "Shit," Jason curses from above me. An eternity later, he joins me on the floor. "Shhh, Brynn. I'm sorry. I didn't mean... You just freaked me out. I... Shit, baby, you can't tell anyone. I love you so much and hate to say this to you, but you can't tell anyone. You have to get rid of the baby and no one can know it's mine."

He wraps his arms around me, pulling me to his lap. God, I want to feel safe here, the way he's always made me. This is the Jason I know. The one who's calm, sweet, and loving, not this man flip-flopping between anger and affection that I'm seeing now.

"Shh...don't cry. I'm sorry. I love you. I just... I wanted you so much, that I couldn't stop myself from lying. One look at you and I was a goner. When I found out how old you are... I did it for us."

You can't tell anyone...

"I couldn't lose you, but don't you see? This is serious

shit. You don't want me to go to jail for loving you, right?" His words are a blur, a muffled echo in my head.

You have to get rid of the baby and no one can know it's mine.

My mom died, and now he wants me to kill our baby. Don't know if I can do it. *Baby… Pregnant. No one can know it's mine.* "What are you talking about?"

"Oh, Brynn. You're so beautiful. Stop crying. I can't handle hearing you cry. I'm so sorry, but you can't be mad at me for loving you. That's why I did it. You love me, too, don't you? If you do, you have to get rid of the baby and not tell anyone. I'll pay for it. I don't want to lose you."

If Jason can't accept what happened, how can I expect Dad to? He'll hate me. Be disappointed. He's already broken because of Mom. "I love you, too," I whisper. "But…" I don't think I can do it. Kill my baby? Kill our baby?

"How far are you?"

"Seven weeks…"

"It's okay. It's not a baby yet. You can do this, Brynn. Do it for us."

My stomach cramps. I just want to go to sleep. Want this to all be some kind of dream.

"I'm not mad that you knew," he continues. "People sometimes lie when they love someone so much. That's why I did it at first. We can keep on pretending like we have been. Keep being happy. I'm only twenty-three. It's not like it's that big a deal."

Twenty-three, twenty-three, twenty-three. The urge to throw up climbs into my throat again. Dizziness sweeps through me. "Jason?"

"Red, you have to trust me. It will work out. You're my beautiful. My beautiful, Red. Don't take that away from me. We'll be okay... It's not a baby yet, anyway."

Each and every one of his words stabs into me at once. I don't know which to focus on. Can't make myself pick any. Love mixes with lies and there's a part of us inside me and he says it's not real. He wants me to get rid of it.

My body takes over and I'm scrambling away from him.

Jason walks toward me, but I can't make myself back away any more. "Don't pretend you didn't know, Brynn. How could you not? I played your game because it made you feel better, but you know who I am. You always knew how old I was. Everyone else will know it, too. They'll know you wanted to trap me. Or they'll think you lied about your age. You wanted an older guy because you were messed up after your mom died. It happens all the time." He shrugs.

"You'd tell them I lied?" He said he loves me, but now he'd tell them I wasn't honest about my age...

It hits me, knocking the air out of me, how much I don't know this Jason, when he says, "Get rid of it and I won't have to." He's so to-the-point. So cold that I don't know if I want to keep crying or hurt him. I can't believe I fell for him.

"I hate you!" I yell. They're the most immature words in the world, but they're all I have. "I *hate* you, Jason!" Stumbling, I run toward the door, but he grabs my arm. A pain shoots through my stomach. My eyes water. My ears feel full, almost echoey.

"You'll break your dad's heart. He'll know his little baby is sleeping around and got knocked up. That you lied to sleep with a local baseball player. After losing your mom, can you do that to him? Everyone else will hate you for trying to trap me, too. Do you want that? Do you want everyone to know you're a slut?"

I rip my arm away from him, covering my mouth with a shaking hand. He's right. I know he's right. *Everyone will hate you.* Haven't I lost enough?

It'll be my word against his.

Jason... I love him, but he never loved me. How will I tell my dad? How will I be a mom?

"Be smart, Brynn. I swear to God, you'd better be smart and get rid of it."

Ignoring his words, I run from the house. I don't remember driving home. I don't remember starting a fire in the woodstove and throwing in that stupid red dress. All I remember are his words. He doesn't love me. Never loved me. He saw someone young and naive and he used me. He wants me to kill the baby.

I know I can't, but I never get the chance anyway. The cramps start in the middle of the night. The rush of blood quickly afterward.

Dad hears me crying.

He takes me to the hospital.

His anger came the next day. The yelling, the disappointment.

He hasn't looked at me the same ever since. No one has.

Jason was right.

INK IS THICKER THAN WATER
by Amy Spalding

In her family, Kellie Brooks has always been stuck in the middle, overlooked and impermanent. Reconnecting with Oliver, the sweet and sensitive college guy she had a near hookup with last year, changes that. Oliver is intense and attractive, and she's sure he's totally out of her league, but soon things are spiraling out of her control. It'll take a new role on the school newspaper and a new job at her mom's tattoo shop for Kellie to realize that defining herself both outside and within her family is what can finally allow her to feel permanent, just like a tattoo.

CHAPTER ONE

Where are you? I need you. (If you have time.)

I shove my phone into my pocket instead of responding to the very unlike-my-sister text Sara has just sent. My best friend is in emergency mode, and I am best-friending.

"But if what Chelsea heard was *true*, why would he be talking to *her*?" Kaitlyn stares at herself in the bathroom mirror and then spins away from her reflection. "We're not even supposed to *be here*, and if he's just going to talk to *her* all night—"

"No one cares that we're here," I say, even though I have no proof of that fact. I'm not letting Kaitlyn panic. "It's a party. People go to parties. We can be people who go to parties now. Or at least bathrooms of parties."

"Ha, ha." She gets her phone out of her purse and checks it. For what, I don't know, but whatever she's hoping for isn't there. "Seriously, Kellie, what am I supposed to do now?"

Here's the thing: I don't really know. But I will be The Friend with The Plan. "Probably we should get out of the bathroom. And you should just go walk in his sightline."

"'Walk in his sightline'?"

"Kaitlyn," I say like this is all so obvious and I'm not just making things up as I go. "He supposedly told a bunch of people you were hot. Go be hot in front of him. He'll stop talking to Brandy about whatever popular people bond over. He will make out with you."

Kaitlyn peers even more intensely into the mirror. "You promise?"

If I'm honest, I'll admit that lately I don't exactly love gazing into mirrors where both Kaitlyn and I are reflected back. It's been years since our bodies had first gotten the memo about grown-up things like boobs and hips, but now that we're well into being sixteen, things seemed to have settled, and I guess we're just going to look like this.

That memo circulating in Kaitlyn's hormones must have used lots of references to the magazines she reads (and I don't because Mom thinks they set bad examples and expectations for teenage girls). Kaitlyn emerged from puberty with a tiny waist and the perfect bra size: not flat-chested but not so developed people make up unfounded rumors about her experience level. Meanwhile, my hormones had taken that memo very literally. Boobs, check, hips, check, two of each and all in the right places.

A renaissance painting for Kaitlyn. Artless puberty for me.

Not that I'm Ugly McUggerstein or anything. Up until very recently, it balanced out, because Kaitlyn always had very normal brown hair that just sort of hung there, the way normal hair does. I'm pretty sure my hair's texture had up until my birth only been seen on lions' manes and expensive stuffed animals, but at least Mom dyes it for me. Currently, it's flamey red and combed through with enough vanilla-scented styling product to behave. From enough of a distance, I absolutely look like I have beautiful, flowing, naturally vanilla-scented red hair.

Lately, though, Kaitlyn has been taking the Amex her parents gave her to make up for getting divorced or whatever to a fancy salon where she emerges with sleek caramel-colored hair that rests above her shoulders with a thoughtful little flip. The first time I saw the new style I told her it looked like angels had patted the ends into place with a flap of their wings. Yeah, that was a joke, but it really did look that flawless. No one prepares you for waking up to realize your best friend who grew up with you step by step and side by side is suddenly, okay, hot.

Also, I should clarify that I hate that I hate this. I am not the kind of person who's ever cared about being the hottest or coolest or most congenial or whatever girls are supposed to get hung up over. So having up my hackles because Kaitlyn now ranks above me in these categories isn't exactly a shining achievement for me.

"I promise," I say, even though I know it's dangerous making promises about another person's actions. This one's as safe a bet as you can get, though. Of course Garrett will want to make out with Kaitlyn! I start to open the bathroom door, but my phone buzzes again in my pocket.

It's another text from Sara: *K? Are you there?*

"Go!" I ignore the text, put my hands on Kaitlyn's shoulders, and steer her toward the door. "Conquer!"

"Hang on." She pulls the strap of her (black, lacy) bra out from her shirt (also black, lacy). "You saw this, right? It's okay? Like, if we get that far?"

"Trust me. Boys will be happy to just see your underwear. I wear frigging boy shorts, and I've had no complaints." I say it so easily by now that it's basically no longer a lie. "Seriously, go do this."

Kaitlyn gives me a hug before flinging open the door of the bathroom. I follow her out, but since I'm only at this party for moral support, I now have nothing to do. I find an open spot on the couch in the living room of whoever's house this is and get my phone back out. *r u ok??* I finally text Sara. *kinda stuck at this party right now.* I don't add that Sara's never not okay because it's probably not nice to make people justify their not-being-okay-ness.

Sara texts back fast: *Sorry about that. I sounded so dramatic! I'm fine.*

This is a Cool Person party, and Kaitlyn and I are definitely not Cool People. I figured I'd be exerting a lot of energy trying to just blend in, but it doesn't actually look any different than any other party I've been to. No one's circling up to take a gulp from the golden chalice of popularity.

"Hey!" Jessie Weinberg, a girl I kind of know from my Literature of an Emerging America class, sits down next to me as I'm texting Sara to make sure she's actually fine. Ticknor Day School isn't big enough not to know everyone—if not by name, at least by face. "I just wanted to tell you that I read your piece and it was *hilarious*."

"My English paper on Mark Twain?" It does not seem possible for a short biographical assignment to be *hilarious*.

"Oh, no, your thing for the *Ticknor Voice*. I know it's not public yet, but Jennifer couldn't shut up about how funny it was."

"Thanks," I say even though I hadn't been trying to be funny. When I saw the flyers for our school newspaper's op/ed column, it just felt *right*. I've been just fine not caring too much about anything for a long time, but that's starting to feel like it's a size too small for me now. I worked as hard as I could on my submission. But I guess if it's funny, whatever works! "Wait, does that mean I'm going to be the new op/ed writer?"

Jessie makes a face like she's thinking, *awkward!* "I probably shouldn't talk about it."

I make the *awkward!* face, too. This makes her laugh, so I guess whatever's up with the paper isn't too big of a deal. And it's so weird I care. I was convinced not caring too much about stuff kept you sane, but lately this tiny voice in my head says it wouldn't be the worst thing in the world.

…Not a literal voice, of course. I'm trying out for an extracurricular, not developing a second personality.

"Kellie." Kaitlyn runs into the room and yanks me to my feet. "We have to go."

"Hey, Kaitlyn," Jessie says.

"Hi, Jessie," Kaitlyn says, then, "Bye, Jessie," and I'm pulled out of the room and then the front door. "Let's go. Tonight's the worst. Tonight is a *disaster*."

"Okay." I don't ask anything, just get her to my car as she starts crying. We sit there for a while in the darkness, and when my phone buzzes again, I leave it and wait.

"He didn't even say hi to me," Kaitlyn says finally. "And then he started making out with Brandy. Like I wasn't even there or didn't even *matter*."

"He's an idiot, then," I say. "Brandy's pretty, but you're…*pretty*. And that whole crowd is made up of idiots. You could do way better."

Now that the silence is broken, I take the opportunity to check my phone. *Yes, I'm sure I'm fine. We're at South City Diner if you want to meet us after your party.*

"Want to meet up with Sara and her friends?" I ask even though I already know the answer and am already turning on the car.

"Help me fix my makeup," she says.

"Your makeup's unfixable! Just go with the badass smeary-eyed look. It works on you."

Kaitlyn laughs and flicks me in the head—*ow*—and hopefully that means stupid Garrett Miller is forgotten for now. And also hopefully the crowd Sara's with at the diner includes her boyfriend and his friends, and Kaitlyn can find a new distraction to get her through the evening.

I drive east on Highway 44 all the way to South Grand, where it feels like I spend as much time as I do in Webster Groves, the suburb of St. Louis where we live. Parking can be crowded, especially on weekends, but I'm so used to the side streets that I zip around and slide into a spot on Hartford almost immediately. When we walk in, the diner's so packed I can't even spot Sara, but Kaitlyn does and pulls me over to the table crowded with, yes, Sara, Sara's boyfriend Dexter, and a bunch of other guys.

"Good evening, ladies," Dexter says, affecting an old-timey accent. "How is this beautiful Saturday treating you and yours?"

Sara and I tell each other almost everything, but we don't really talk about guys—who knows why—and so that was only one of the reasons I was surprised when she started going out with Dexter. Wasn't my perfect pre-prelaw sister way too serious for stuff like boys and dating when she was studying her butt off and worrying about college applications? And if I *had* been forced into describing the kind of guy Sara would end up with, I would not have said *redheaded hipster hottie*. But then all of a sudden, Dexter was a thing.

Dexter is a senior at the all-boys school Chaminade, where he wears his uniform tie slightly askew and heads up both the Young Democrats Club and the Poetry in Action Club, the latter of which he'd also founded. (No one really seems to know what Poetry in Action actually *is*. Poetry seems like a pretty passive activity. Sometimes Dexter recites Yeats really loud and in public. Is that it?)

Anyway, I guess it works because they *are* serious, about each other and about the stuff in their lives. They study together and talk nonstop about college and go to lectures and museums and foreign films. Even when Dexter's doing goofy accents or shouting poetry at the stars, Sara looks at him like it all makes sense to her. The lesson I take from this is that love is finding someone who thinks everything about you that's weird is actually hot.

"Make room for Kellie and Kaitlyn," Sara says, and the guy on her other side jumps at her command by shoving in two chairs for us. Kaitlyn's immediately eyeing the other prospects, but I stare Sara down until she notices.

"What's up with you?" she asks like she didn't send me two emergency-ish texts less than an hour ago.

"You're sure you're okay?"

"Don't I look okay?" she asks with a smile. And *of course* she does, because Sara is basically two steps shy of a supermodel. Tall and blond and the kind of cheekbones that people comment on. Four separate times people have asked Sara if they saw her in a Macy's ad. (No, but that seems like a pretty good compliment.)

"We can talk later if you want," I say even though that's the kind of thing she says to me and never vice versa. Sara's only a year older than me, but she's got it *together*.

"Sure." She turns her attention back to Dexter, who's in the midst of some elaborate story about a fight he witnessed between two stray cats. Kaitlyn's talking with the guy on her other side, so I finally glance all the way around our table.

Across from me, sitting just a few people down—like it's *normal*!—is Oliver.

Oliver! Dexter's brother. Who knows a lot about me. Who knows things I don't want anyone else knowing. Who I hoped would have found a way to text me even though I'd never given him my number and even though the thought made me a little terrified.

Oliver.

He raises his eyebrows at me and grins. And I don't know what I'm doing any more than I did back in May when everything happened—or, well, didn't happen. But I can't help it. I grin back.

Discover our digital first books for teens from Embrace...

SIDELINED
by Kendra C. Highley

After being pushed to excel her entire life, high school basketball star Genna Pierce is finally where she wants to be. University scouts are taking notice, her team is on its way to the state tourney, and Jake Butler, the hot boy she's daydreamed about since ninth grade, is showing some *definite* interest. When he asks her out and their relationship takes off, Genna believes things can't get better.

Then, it's over.

A freak accident ends her career before it's even begun. Her parents are fighting more than ever, her friends don't understand what she's going through, and she's not sure who she is without basketball. And while he tries to be there for her, Genna doesn't understand how Jake could ever want the broken version of the girl he fell for.

Her life in a tailspin, Genna turns to the only solace that eases her pain: Vicodin.

WHERE YOU'LL FIND ME
by Erin Fletcher

When Hanley Helton discovers a boy living in her garage, she knows she should kick him out. But Nate is too charming to be dangerous. He just needs a place to get away, which Hanley understands. Her own escape methods—vodka, black hair dye, and pretending the past didn't happen—are more traditional, but who is she to judge?

Nate doesn't tell her why he's in her garage, and she doesn't tell him what she's running from. Soon, Hanley's trading her late-night escapades for all-night conversations and stolen kisses. But when Nate's recognized as the missing teen from the news, Hanley isn't sure which is worse: that she's harboring a fugitive, or that she's in love with one.

MADE OF STARS
by Kelley York

When eighteen-year-old Hunter Jackson and his half sister, Ashlin, return to their dad's for the first winter in years, they expect everything to be just like the warmer months they'd spent there as kids. And it is—at first. But Chance, the charismatic and adventurous boy who made their summers epic, is harboring deep secrets. Secrets that are quickly spiraling into something else entirely.

The reason they've never met Chance's parents or seen his home is becoming clearer. And what the siblings used to think of as Chance's quirks— the outrageous stories, his clinginess, his dangerous impulsiveness—are now warning signs that something is seriously off.

Then someone turns up with a bullet to the head, and all eyes shift to Chance's family. Hunter and Ashlin know Chance is innocent...they just have to prove it. But how can they protect the boy they both love when they can't trust a word Chance says?

In the Blood
by Sara Hantz

For seventeen years, Jed Franklin's life was normal. Then his father was charged with the abuse and murder of four young boys and *normal* became a nightmare.

His mom's practically a walking zombie, he's lost most of his friends, and the press camps out on his lawn. The only things that keep him sane are his little sis; his best friend and dream girl, Summer; and the alcohol he stashes in his room. But after Jed wakes up from a total blackout to discover a local kid has gone missing—a kid he was last seen talking to—he's forced to face his greatest fear: that he could somehow be responsible.

In a life that's spiraled out of control, Jed must decide if he chooses his own destiny with Summer by his side or if the violent urges that plagued his father are truly in the blood...

Olivia Twisted
by Vivi Barnes

Olivia

He tilts my chin up so my eyes meet his, his thumb brushing lightly across my lips. I close my eyes. I know Z is trouble. I know that being with him is going to get me into trouble. I don't care.

At least at this moment, I don't care.

Tossed from foster home to foster home, Olivia's seen a lot in her sixteen years. She's hardened, sure, though mostly just wants to fly under the radar until graduation. But her natural ability with computers catches the eye of Z, a mysterious guy at her new school.

Soon, Z has brought Liv into his team of hacker elite—
break into a few bank accounts, and voila, he drives a
motorcycle. Follow his lead, and Olivia might even be
able to escape from her oppressive foster parents. As
Olivia and Z grow closer, though, so does the watchful
eye of Bill Sykes, Z's boss. And he's got bigger plans for
Liv…

Z

I can picture Liv's face: wide-eyed, trusting. Her smooth
lips that taste like strawberry Fanta.

It was just a kiss. That's all. She's just like any other
girl.

Except that she's not.

Thanks to Z, Olivia's about to get twisted.